LARRY 2: THE SQUEEQUEL

Adam Millard is the author of twenty-nine novels, seventeen novellas, and more than two hundred short stories, which can be found in various anthologies and magazine. His work has been translated for the Spanish, German, and Russian Markets. Adam Lives in Newcastle-under-Lyme with his wife, Dawn, and their two cats, Butter and Toast.

LARRY 2: THE SQUEEQUEL

ADAM MILLARD

Copyright © 2015 Adam Millard

This Edition Published 2024 by Crowded Quarantine Publications

The moral right of the author has been asserted

All characters in this publication are fictitious and any resemblance to real persons, living or dead, is purely coincidental.

All rights reserved.
No part of this publication may be reproduced, stored in a retrieval system, or transmitted, in any form or by any means without the prior permission in writing of the publisher, nor be otherwise circulated in any form of binding or cover other than that in which it is published and without a similar condition including this condition being imposed on the subsequent purchase.

A CIP catalogue record for this book is available from the British Library

ISBN 978-1-7384764-5-9

Printed and bound in Great Britain

Crowded Quarantine Publications Ltd.

For Butter and Toast. My cats, not the breakfast food.

LARRY II: THE SQUEEQUEL

"Is there any chance this shit will be a trilogy? Only I've always fancied being in 3D." – Larry *"Pigface"* Travers

1
Camp Diamond Creek 2015

The sheriff trundled through the forest. Trundling had become the new walking, you see. If you weren't trundling, you might as well have been standing still. Some people preferred to *saunter*, but not this sheriff. This sheriff was on a mission, and missions such as his required a little urgency, the kind of urgency that one could only get with a trundle. Of course, one could traipse, but there's something pretentious about traipsing, and pretention, like millions of other words, was not in the sheriff's vocabulary.

For almost a year Sheriff Tobin had been searching for a cabin. That wasn't to say he was looking for a nice holiday home, a place in the woods in which he could vacation with his wife and dog. He *was*, but that's another story entirely. You could probably read *that* story in *Sheriff's Shanties*, or *Cop Campsites*. If you are really desperate, *Marshall Lodges* ran an article about

Sheriff Tobin six years back in which he professed to enjoying jazz and eating enchiladas, though not at the same time, that's just dangerous. Tobin didn't like to do dangerous things, not unless it would progress his career, which was why he was now trundling – not traipsing or sauntering – through a dark forest in the middle of the night.

Sheriff Tobin was afraid of the dark. And forests petrified him; especially petrified forests. How could anyone feel comfortable setting foot in a wood which was equally afraid of you setting foot in it? No, petrified forests were a no-no, as were panicked plantations and horrifying holts. He could just about stomach a spine-chilling spinney, if the money was right, but you would have to catch him on a good day, and those were rare.

This was not a good day. Sure, he had won a dollar on a two-dollar scratch-card, and he'd managed to keep his handlebar moustache symmetrical, at least until lunchtime (two rounds of prawn sandwich and half a cucumber), but apart from that, much like the assassination of JFK or the time Billy Ray and Tish Cyrus decided to give parenthood another chance, the day was one to forget.

"Pigface," Sheriff Tobin muttered. Muttering

LARRY II: THE SQUEEQUEL

was the new mumbling. Of course, people sputtered, but sputtering involved spittle, and in that moment Sheriff Tobin's mouth was like Gandhi's flip-flop – dry, and beige. Very beige. If you were to put Sheriff Tobin's tongue next to Gandhi's flip-flop, well, you would be classed as insane, but on top of that, you would find it hard to differentiate between the two. It's amazing how similes work, isn't it?

Sheriff Tobin should have finished work at eight and, in fact, he *did*, inasmuch as he wasn't being paid for this little detour on his way home. He had clocked out at the station along with all the other cops. All the other cops were already at home, eating TV dinners and supping from filthy beakers or fornicating with their fat wives and pretending it was okay to do so because life was life and their lives were awful. Those cops didn't saunter, nor did they traipse or trundle; they limped. Several of them had hernias. One of them was missing an eye and at least three of them had breathing difficulties. It came with the job, if you were to replace the word 'job' with the words 'philandering with an obese spouse'. Sheriff Tobin's wife was not overweight. At least, not if he blew her up at regular intervals.

"Fucking *Pigface*," he said once again, stepping over a log and landing in a pile of wild boar shit. After that it was almost impossible to trundle. At best he could falter, though it was more of a hobble, and hobbling was not something he had prepared for. He had prepared for a waddle, if the worst came to the worst, but this…well, this was just a clusterfuck.

And then he saw it. The cabin in the woods. The thing he had been searching for, and it was more decrepit than he had imagined it would be. It was so run-down that renowned realtor, Brian Bosworth, would have taken one look at it, whistled, and then run off into the trees, screaming at the top of his lungs. Brian Bosworth wasn't much of a traipser, nor a trundler. He knew a shithole when he saw one, and *this*, well, this was a shithole of epic proportions.

"*Pigface's* house," the sheriff said, slapping his lips together and slowing to an amble. Ambles were there for when trundling became a chore. You could amble all day, so long as you'd remembered to bring a picnic and a good book. "I don't fucking believe it."

And he *didn't!* All this time he had been looking for it, and there it was, in plain sight. The house

LARRY II: THE SQUEEQUEL

that Jack built. Jack didn't build it. Larry 'Pigface' *Travers* built it; Jack just held the cement and, occasionally, ordered an unhealthy sandwich of a lunchtime. Jack has an entire backstory that deserves a book of its own, but this is Larry's story, and Larry's the one holding the bricks…

"I need backup." Sheriff Tobin slowed to a halt a few yards from the front door of the decrepit cabin. Somewhere, not too far away, a pig *souieeed*, which was amazing really considering all the vowels. Reaching into his off-duty uniform – which was almost identical to his on-duty uniform, except for the gun and handcuffs – Tobin located his walkie-talkie and pulled it from his waistband.

Holding it to his mouth, he depressed the button on the walkie's side (though not with tales of fat wives or petrified forests) and began to speak.

"Come in," he said. "Come in, this is Sheriff Tobin. Might I have a cheeky word with you about something I've just trundled upon?"

It took a few seconds, but a voice responded, and Tobin recognised the voice as that of Desk-Sergeant Bradley. "Sheriff Tobin? Shouldn't you be at home by now?"

"I came out for a trundle," Tobin said. "Turned

into an amble, but that's beside the point. You'll never believe where I am."

There was a slight pause on the other end of the line as Desk-Sergeant Bradley had a jolly good think. "Is it Narnia?" he finally said, "because I would never believe you were in Narnia."

Tobin made his way around the back of the cabin, being careful not to tread on anything that went *crack!* or *snap!*. It was a lot harder than it sounded. The ground was peppered with objects whose sole purpose was to give away his position. "It's not Narnia," he whispered. "Have another go, but do it quietly. I'm in stealth mode."

"Is it Mordor?" said Desk-Sergeant Bradley. "I only ask because my daughter is a huge fan, and she'd lose her shit if I could get her Christopher Lee's autograph. Failing that, one of the hobbitses will do."

"I'm not in Mordor," Tobin whispered as he approached the rear entry of the cabin (not a euphemism). "Think a little closer to home."

Another slight pause, and then, "You're not in Mrs Palmer's house, are you. She gets ever so funny about intruders, especially at this time of night."

Mrs Palmer, Tobin knew, was Desk-Sergeant

LARRY II: THE SQUEEQUEL

Bradley's next-door neighbour. He knew this because they had been called to her address on many occasions, usually to sort out an intruder, normally in the middle of the night. "Why the bloody hell would I be in Mrs Palmer's house?"

"Why would you be in *Mordor*?" replied Desk-Sergeant Bradley, with more than a soupcon of derision in his tone. "Look, we could be at this all night. Why don't you just tell me where you are, and I can either believe you, or tell you to piss off before slamming down the phone in anger, and before you say anything, I know it's not a phone. Let's just pretend it is for argument's sake."

The pig, off in the distance, *soueeeeed* again. There was no other word for the noise which escaped Sheriff Tobin in reply. That word was fart. "You remember all those murders last year up at Camp Diamond Creek?"

"Oh, *yeah*. That guy in the pig mask, and all that nonsense. I found the whole thing very difficult to believe. I mean, if that were a book, and I could read, I'd have probably given up on it by the third act."

"*Chapter*," Tobin said.

"What?"

"In books you don't have acts. You have

chapters. In posh books you have Roman numerals, and if you're reading The Bible, you have a whole heap of numbers and letters, so that those schooled in the art of Bible-recitation can toss the chapter code back at you when they've finished spouting religious doctrine. Acts are for plays."

"But I don't like *plays*," Desk-Sergeant Bradley said. "I like *porn*. Do you know anything about porn?"

"Look, I'm standing outside a ramshackle cabin in the middle of the fucking woods here," Tobin said. "It's got to be *his*!"

"Whose?"

"The Pigface!"

"I think it's just *Pigface*," said Desk-Sergeant Bradley with a hearty sigh. "The 'The' makes him sound like a supervillain, like *The Joker*, or *The Bin Laden*."

Sheriff Tobin stopped just short of the rear entry (still not a euphemism) and drew his weapon, which happened to be a set of keys, and not keys to something cool like a Lamborghini or a penthouse suite at The Ritz. They were keys to his beat-up Volvo. The keyring hanging from the loop (a stainless steel Mickey Mouse head) was probably worth more than the car. The loop was probably worth more than the car. "I'm about to go in," he whispered.

"Don't do *that*," Desk-Sergeant Bradley said, eschewing the whisper for a much more useful holler. Tobin held the walkie to his chest to stifle the racket. "I'll send backup. Where are you?"

Tobin looked around. "I'm standing in the woods in front of a rundown cabin."

"You're going to have to be more specific," said Desk-Sergeant Bradley. "Have a good look around. Can you see anything distinguishing?"

"What, like a rabbit in a waistcoat?" Tobin replied. "There's nothing but trees."

The sound of keys clacking emerged from the walkie-talkie. Sheriff Tobin sighed with relief. "Thank God," he said. "You're trying to fathom my location."

"Erm, yes, that's precisely what I'm doing. I'm not searching for porn, no, not on your nelly."

"You're searching for porn, aren't you?" Tobin shook his head and closed his eyes, which was a terrible thing to do if you were standing on the front porch – or the ramshackle equivalent – of a renowned serial killer. When he opened his eyes again, he found himself face to face with a hunched figure wearing a pig-mask. He could just about make out the eyes through the thin slits of the mask. Rheumy eyes, they were. The kind of eyes that had seen *stuff*. They say that eyes are the windows to the soul, but these eyes weren't. These eyes were the windows to hell.

"Is that an axe?" Tobin said, pointing to the axe in the maniac's hand and answering his own question in the process. "Are you going to kill me now?"

The Pigface, or just *Pigface* according to Desk-Sergeant Bradley, shrugged: *You've not left me much of a choice, have you? Rocking up here in the dead of night.*

"Are you still *there*, Tobin?" Desk-Sergeant Bradley said. His voice might as well have been a million miles away, for all the good it did. "Do you know anything about hermaphrodites, only I'm on this website and the place is *teeming* with them?"

Now, Sheriff Tobin knew a thing or two about hermaphrodites, such as you should never tell one to go fuck itself as they're always happy to oblige, but there were more important things afoot.

Like death.

Death was afoot.

And Sheriff Tobin did what any sane man would do when faced with his own demise. He shat his pants, made a strange noise right at the back of his throat, and hoped there was an afterlife, with or without virgins for him to defile.

"Tobin?" Desk-Sergeant Bradley sounded uneasy, which was amazing, really, as he wasn't the one about to be chopped up into small pieces and fed to the pig.

"I don't suppose you'd take a bribe?" said the Sheriff, appealing to the better nature of the maniac standing before him, but that was the thing with murderous butchers; they never seemed to possess a better nature.

"Souuuueeeeeee!" said Pigface, and brought the axe around in a wide arc. There was a meaty thud, and then things seemed to move over and over for Sheriff Tobin, as if he was cartwheeling through the woods like an overjoyed gazelle.

Souuuueeee? he thought as his decapitated head thunked against a tree-trunk and came to a rolling-stop in the undergrowth. Surely that should have been '*squeeeeeee*', he thought, frowning.

As final thoughts went, it wasn't great, and so he quickly flicked through his wank-bank and arrived at a rather gratuitous image of pre-muscle dysmorphia Madonna. Needless to say, Sheriff Tobin still died with a frown upon his face.

2
The Travers Cabin

The man sat shivering in the semi-dark of the cabin, wandering what the hell was going on, and how long it would be before the old dear with the strange smell offered him a cup of something warm. In the corner of the room, a fireplace lay empty. *What's the bleeding point of it?* the man thought. *It's not as if she's short of wood; she fucking lives in one, for starters.*

"Sorry about that," said the woman, returning from whatever it was she had been doing. "I ain't kiddin' you, that's about the third Sheriff I've 'ad to deal with this week. We're only on Tuesday!" She slapped a bloody axe and a strange, half-melted pig mask down on the table next to the pile of severed limbs, and turned to the man with an expectant look upon her wizened face. "So what d'ya reckon?"

The man, whose name shall be revealed shortly, shrugged. "About what?" he said. "You haven't asked me anything yet."

"Oh, that's right," said the woman. "Honestly, I think I'd forget my ass if it wasn't nailed to my pussy." She cackled, and as she did, her eyes seemed to roll around in their sockets as if they were independent of her. The man turned his attention to the fireplace until the woman had composed herself. "So what d'ya reckon?" she said.

"I reckon you should get some wood for that fire," said the man, whose name shall be revealed shortly. "It's colder than an Eskimo's chuff in here."

"'Ere, you ain't from the gas-board, is ya?" said the woman, whose name shall be revealed in the following sentence. "'cause Edie Travers don't take kindly to utilities and those what peddle 'em." Told you.

"You *know* I'm not from the gas-board," said the man. "You called *me*, remember?"

"But what if you was a wrong number?" said Edie.

"Look, this joke's gone on for far too long. Can we just get to the meat of the matter?" he said, waving his hands frantically in the air for no good reason.

Edie rolled a cigarette between fingers that looked like twiglets, and very well might have been, before saying, "You's that voodoo-man, ain'tcha? The one what brought back that serial killer in a ginger midget's body over in Chicago?"

The man, whose name will be revealed extremely soon, leaned back in his chair and sighed. How could this keep happening? "Dr. Death?" said the man. "You wanted *Dr.* Death, and it wasn't a ginger midget, it was a child's plaything, and from what I understand, that little dungaree-bastard's still out there." He waved his hands again, this time finishing off with a couple of jabs in Edie's direction.

Edie frowned. "Why'd'ya keep doing that?" she said.

"Doing *what?*" said the man. He stood from the table, kicked out at the air a couple of times, and then sat back down again.

"That!" said Edie. "Doing all that nonsense!"

"This is the third one, isn't it?" the man said, whipping out an elbow. "The third ones are always in 3D."

"This is the *second* one!" Edie said, shaking her head. "I should imagine the third 'un will foller this 'un."

"Oh," said the man, sheepishly.

"Anyway, never mind all that!" Edie said, gnawing nervously on her roll-yer-own. "If you're not Dr. Death, who the hell are *you*, then? You better not be from the gas-board—"

"I'm *Roger* Death!" said Roger Death. "*Dr.* Death was my little brother, God rest his soul."

"But'cha do voodoo?" Edie said, more hopeful than anything. "I mean, that's the kind of job what runs in the family, ain't it?"

"I'm a *carpet*-cleaner," Roger Death said. "And since you don't have any carpets, there isn't much I can do for you."

Edie Travers seemed to weaken in that moment. Her head fell forward; she was only an inch away from taking a severely-decayed finger to the eye. "Why din'tcha tell me that on the phone?" she wailed. "I got me 'opes up that you was gonna bring back my Larry, and *now* look. I've made a right mess of me table-cloth with all these limbs."

"I've got my gear in the van," said Roger Death, never one to turn down an opportunity. "Carpets, table-cloths, curtains, it's all the same, really."

But Edie Travers wasn't listening, for Edie Travers was wailing like a newborn baby, occasionally picking up one of the rotten limbs from the table and giving it a sniff. She sounded, Roger Death thought, like his PowerVac 5000™ (other high-powered vacuum-cleaners are available).

"Oooooohhhhh!" she moaned. "Ooooooohhhh, it was going to be so special. I've got a lovely broth on the stove, and the chicken only just fit in the oven, and now it's all gonna go to waste! Oooohhh, woe is me! Woe is me, etcetera, etcetera, and so on, and so forth!"

Now Roger Death, who hadn't eaten since nine of that very same a.m. and whose stomach was now growling up a fierce one, had never been very good at voodoo, not like his brother Doc, but the thought of missing out on a decent repast before setting back for the city offended him. *I mean*, he thought, *what could possibly go wrong?*

"I'll have a go," said Roger.

"You what?" said Edie, pulling a severed finger from between her puckered lips.

"I, erm..." Roger glanced down at the vast array of body parts. Putting them back together with voodoo, and in the correct place, would be like trying to complete a Su-Doku puzzle blindfolded, and without the aid of a pen. But he'd gone and said it now. If only he could figure out what to say next. "Why did your, erm, *son* have seven arms and three legs?" That would have to do.

LARRY II: THE SQUEEQUEL

"Don't be daft," said Edie. "Some of these ain't his, 'specially that black one there, and that one with the butterfly tattoo."

Roger was about to ask who, if not her son, they belonged to, then decided the resultant explanation would cut into his chicken- and soup-eating time, so he decided against it. "And a head?" he said. "I'm assuming your son had one when he was alive?"

"You taking the piss?" said Edie. "Course he 'ad a head. How do you think he brushed his teeth?"

Confused, and rightly so, but not altogether put off, Roger stood from the chair and paced the length of the room. It wasn't a huge room, but it was large enough to pace. Pacing was something Roger Death was good at, but that was only because he hadn't had a crack at trundling yet. "I have had a little experience in voodoo and the like," he said. "My brother might have been better at it than me, but I was definitely worse at it than him."

It was Edie's turn to be confused; she did so by grinding her roll-yer-own into her temple.

"Oh, Doc and I used to bring dead things back to life all the *time*." He smiled and gazed off into the distance, as if in fond remembrance; he would have gazed a lot further had the cabin wall not prevented him from doing so. "Cats, 'coons, insects. Momma said we'd best stop bringing dead shit back to life. She said it would come back to haunt us, that dead is dead, and it's best left as such." His smile faltered. "Pity, really, as the next thing to die was Momma, God rest her soul."

"Is there a point to this, or can we just get Larry up and about again?" Edie stood and limped (she couldn't trundle if her life depended on it) across the room.

"The last time I did this, I had the whole body to work with." He motioned to the table and the pile of limbs. "If he comes back without a head, I can't make any promises he'll last the night." Heads, as it were, are extremely important. You could have the most beautiful body in the world, but without a head, you'd look a little iffy.

"Just do what you 'ave to do, and we'll see what's what," said Edie. "I'll go and check on the soup, leave you two alone for a bit." She ran a cold, arthritic hand down his arm before heading for the door. "'Ere," she said, turning back. "You ain't one of them funny fuckers what likes to fiddle with folk after they've gone?"

LARRY II: THE SQUEEQUEL

"What, like Calista Flockhart?" Roger had never been so offended in his entire life. So offended was he that it would take three bowls of soup later on to forgive the demented old sow. "How very dare you!"

"You never know," she said. "You never know." And with that, she turned and limped from the room, leaving Roger Death and the Table of Limbs (not to be confused with Harry Twotter and the Ladle of Pimms) alone, not for the first time that night.

"Right!" said Roger, slapping his hands together and moving toward the table. "Let's have a little looksee, shall we?" He looked, and it didn't take long to arrive at the conclusion that he had bitten off more than he could chew.

A promise is a promise is a promise, and the smell of the soup permeating the cabin jogged something in his memory, something that had, until now, lain dormant. "Yeeeeeesssss," Roger hissed. "That ought to do it." He took a deep breath, closed his eyes, clapped his hands together several times until they were sore, and said, "*Ade due damballa. Give me the power I beg of you. Secoise entienne mais pois de morte. Morteisma lieu de vocuier de mieu vochette, and so on, and so forth, etcetera, etcetera...*"

Adam Millard

Well, it worked in the movies…

LARRY II: THE SQUEEQUEL

3
The Travers Cabin

Movies, Roger Death quickly realised, are awfully different to books. First of all the special effects in books are not as spectacular as their big-screen counterpart. Sure, an author can wax lyrical about blood and guts and monsters from the deep for pages and pages, but Ray Harryhausen could better that with just a tub of Play-Doh and a couple of pipe-cleaners. Secondly, Haitian Creole sounds beautiful on screen, but reading it from a page without skipping to the end of the sentence is almost impossible.

That was the reason why it hadn't worked; even Roger Death had got bored around the halfway point.

"You can do this," he told himself as he jumped up and down on the spot like a hundred-metre sprinter about to go hell-for-leather toward the finishing line.

"Everything going alright in there?" cried Edie from the kitchen. "Is he back together yet. Larry, are you back together yet?"

Roger stared down at the pile of rotten limbs on the table. He certainly wasn't back together yet, not unless he'd looked like a pile of rotten limbs to begin with. "Any minute now!" he answered. "I think I've got to get rid of the ones which aren't his!"

Yes! *That's* what it was. How could he possibly magic a human back together if there were foreign bits present? It's like trying to put a box of puzzle pieces together when no two pieces were from the same puzzle.

"Righty-ho!" said Roger Death, stepping up to the table. "Dum-de-dum-de-aahhh, this one's definitely not his." He picked the mangled leg up and tossed it across the room. "And I'll be damned if this is his." Out went the arm. "And *this* one." He picked it up and…

"*Ow*, you bastard!" Edie said, emerging from the kitchen door. "Throwing *limbs*, are we? Is *that* what I'm paying you for? Look at the bloody mess you're making! I only swept this morning."

Roger Death scrutinised the floor, which hadn't, he surmised, seen a brush since the Wright Brothers had decided that walking was for pussies. "I've figured it out," he said, motioning to the table, upon which now sat the correct number of limbs, an axe, and a half-melted pig-mask.

"That's spiffing," Edie said. "Figured *what*

LARRY II: THE SQUEEQUEL

out?"

"The reason why it wasn't working."

"I didn't know it *wasn't* working," said Edie. "Are you telling me that my Larry's gonna be in four pieces for the rest of 'is life?"

"No, that's the precise *opposite* of what I'm trying to tell you." Roger Death took a deep breath and momentarily closed his eyes. He pitied the guy lying on the table, for his mother was an utter crackerjack; the humane thing would be to leave Larry alone, pretend he couldn't do it, and get the hell out of dodge (though not before a healthy dollop of said crackerjack's special broth. "Did you ever see that film, *Body Parts*?"

"Do you see a television, Sherlock?"

Roger Death sighed. "Okay, well it's about this guy that loses his arm in an accident, but luckily for him, they manage to stick a new one on. Unfortunately, the arm used to belong to a serial killer, and this guy—"

"Other than the fact we're standing here looking down at a bunch of body parts, does this 'ave anything to do with Larry?"

No, it doesn't," said Roger Death. "I'll just crack on with it then, shall I?"

"For the best," said Edie, who wanted her son

back so desperately. There was a pile of rubbish in the kitchen so tall, she'd been talking to it for the last three months. Then there was Wilbur, whose sty hadn't been mucked out since Larry's passing. The saying goes, 'He's as happy as a pig in shit,' but even Wilbur was starting to look pissed off with the state of the place, and Edie was fucked if she was going to clean it.

"Right." Roger Death rolled his sleeves up, not for the first time that night. "And you're sure you don't have the head knocking about the place?"

"I would've noticed it," said Edie.

"Okay. In that case, this scene's gone on for far too long. Let's get cracking." He inhaled deeply, coughed and spluttered until he was blue in the face, made a mental note not to do it again, and said, "*Ade due damballa, give me the power I beg of you…*"

Before he'd finished the first line (a line that will probably, no doubt, almost certainly, cost someone a lawsuit) the limbs on the table began to tremble. Roger Death, of course, didn't see them tremble, for he was in the moment and, truth be told, more than a little terrified to open his eyes.

"*Secoise entienne mais pois de morte,*" said Roger, which was equally as plagiaristic, but he reckoned he could get away with it.

"It's a-workin'," Edie said, mesmerised as the arms and legs began to draw together. "I don't believe it! You're doin' it, you silly carpet-cleaner!"

"*Morteisma lieu de vocuier de mieu vochette,*" Roger said, because in for a penny, in for a pound. "*Endonline pour de boisette damballa! Secoise entienne mais pois de morte. Endelieu pour de boisette damballa!!!*" He dry-swallowed, opened one eye, saw the limbs squirming and writhing upon the table, and quickly closed it again. "I've never seen anything so fucking disgusting in my entire life," said he. "And I was a *choirboy*."

"I think we used that joke in the first book," Edie said. "Anyway, keep it going. We don't want to lose it now, do we?"

Roger Death took a deep breath, for he was an awful glutton for punishment, before pressing on. "*Ade due damballa, give me the power I beg of you…*"

"You've already *done* that bit," Edie said, squeezing his arm.

"It has to be repeated four times," said Roger Death. "And can you not squeeze that part of my arm. I've got a lump and it's sore."

"You should see a doctor about that," Edie said. "Pity your brother isn't still alive."

"Can I continue?"

"I don't know. Can you?"

"*Secoise entienne mais pois de morte. Morteisma lieu de vocuier de mieu vochette.*" By now, the limbs on the table were in full flow. The arms were up onto their elbows, arm-wrestling, which looked as awkward as it sounded, and the legs were kicking one another about the shins. If there had been a head present, it would have almost certainly been belting out the greatest hits of Rod Stewart – both of them. "*Endonline pour de boisette damballa! Secoise entienne mais pois de morte. Endelieu pour de boisette damballa!!!*"

"*Look*!" Edie said. Roger didn't want to, but the old hag was prising his eyelids apart, and before he knew it, he was watching the pig mask as it stretched and moulded itself into a head shape. "See! I told ya we din't need 'is 'ead. The *mask's* 'is 'ead."

For the first time since he'd arrived at the dilapidated cabin in the middle of the woods, Roger Death felt as if he was doing something he shouldn't have been. It was the same feeling he'd had as a child, when his mother caught him with his hand in the cookie jar, and the same feeling he'd had as a teenager, when his father caught him with

LARRY II: THE SQUEEQUEL

his hands down his—

"*Squeeeeeeeeeeeeeeeeeeee!*" the mask screeched as it rolled across the dusty old table, coming to a stop between the severed arms. The sound of bones cracking as they snapped into place reminded Roger of the time he'd had a seizure in a bubble-wrap factory – probably the best place for those kinds of things, safety first, and all that.

A pair of thick shoulders stretched up from the arms and seemed to grasp tightly onto the pig mask as if they were lovers meeting for the first time – an impossibility, but nevertheless, the best description Roger could summon in that moment. With the head in place, a torso began to grow between the lower-arms of the thing, filling out quickly, as if there was a midget beneath the old table, tap-dancing on a foot-pump.

It's terrible! Roger thought. Horrible…so horrible! But the scent of the broth emerging from the kitchen – parsnips, carrots, some sort of meat the likes of which it was best not to ask too many questions about, considering his surroundings and the fact he was trying to reanimate a dead person – was almost unbearable. His head told him to run, RUN! Run and don't look back! But his heart said, "You haven't had parsnips since Christmas."

"I'll just go and check on my parsnips," said Edie, before scampering away to the kitchen. "Give me a yell if he's done before I get back."

Roger looked down at the sinewy veins as they weaved together upon the table, over and under, over and under, like worms trying to figure out whose turn it was to go on top. *I'll go mad soon*, he thought. *Mad, like Gary Busey or The Hoff.*

"Oh God!" Roger said. "I'm going to be eating burgers off the ground. I'm going to be shaving my head and trying to thwack the paparazzi with an umbrella. They're going to throw me in the looney bin!" And he'd heard all about such establishments from his buddy, Razor-Wrist Bill. Dry mashed potato three times a day…reruns of *The Fresh Prince of Bel-Air* on the TV every single waking hour…wardens sneaking into your room at night and rearranging the contents of your sock drawer…if you weren't mad when you went in, you bloody well were when you came out.

"Ya like a dumplin'?" Edie said, leaning against the kitchen doorframe like a geriatric saloon wench.

"*Am* I?" Roger said, unable to take his eyes off the body on the table as it continued to form. "I've never been called one before."

LARRY II: THE SQUEEQUEL

"Would you *like* a dumplin'?" Edie reiterated, licking the wooden spoon in her hand as if it had paid up front for her services, and hadn't been a tight-fisted bugger about it, either. "With yer' broth?"

Roger couldn't fathom what was happening, how she could be so damn calm. "YES I'D LOVE A DUMPLIN'!" he shouted, because that's what any normal person would have done in that moment. Upon the table, one leg clicked into its socket, and the mask said, "*Squeeeeeeeee!*" which was getting to be something of a catchphrase, though not as annoying as "*Nice to see you, to see you nice,*" or "*You are the weakest link. Goodbye.*"

"This isn't right!" Roger Death said, all of a fluster. "Do you have any idea the kind of *abomination* we're invoking here?"

Edie Travers, still fellating the wooden spoon, said, "Well a'course I do. I gave *birth* to the little sumbitch, din't I?" And with that, she spun and ventured back into the kitchen, where parsnips and carrots and questionable meats were simmering together, oblivious that they were about to be served upon the very table that a pile of rotting limbs had recently become a writhing, twitching, stinking, transmuting, heavy-breathing, squeeing, willy-fiddling mess of a man.

"*Squeeeeeee!*" the thing cried. It sounded as if it might be in pain, and Roger Death, in a moment of absurd valour, stepped closer to the table and reached for the axe which lay there.

Surely, putting such a horrible beast out of its misery was in the best interests of all involved parties? Granted, it might result in a reduced serving of broth, and possibly only one dumpling, but separating the thing's still-forming face with an axe was the right thing to do, wasn't it?

"Don't even *think* about it."

Roger whipped his head across, saw the old biddy in the kitchen doorframe, and froze. His hand was almost touching the axe. Just a few more inches and he'd be able to lop the abomination's head off, convince its mother it was for the best, then settle down at the table with a bowl of something warm-but-dubious and a glass of something tepid-and-dirty.

"What happened to the wooden spoon?" he said, motioning to the large blade that had replaced it. Unsurprisingly she wasn't dragging her dark, hairy tongue across this one. "Look, I don't want any trouble, okay? I just want to get out of here and leave you and your boy" – he pointed to the squelching mass on the table – "alone. I'm sure you've got plenty to catch up on. Was he around for *True Detective*?"

"We don't—"

"*Have* a TV," he said, taking tiny steps away from the table. "I know that. Would you like me to run you through the entire first season of—"

"We've never heard of *Breaking Bad*," said she. "You were going to chop 'im up." Her tone suggested she couldn't believe he was capable of such a thing. "You were going to re-chop up my Larry."

"Look at it!" Roger said, gesturing frantically to the writhing form upon the table. "That's not *right*! I never signed up for this. I thought I was going to be giving your hall, stairs, and landing a good once over, not reviving a fucking serial killer, pardon my French."

"*Squeeeeeee!*" the mess upon the table said.

"See. Do you see how *wrong* this is?" Roger Death did. It was a pity he hadn't spotted it a few minutes ago, before he'd started spouting voodoo mantras as if they were going out of fashion.

"You'll sit your ass down and wait until this is done!" yelled Edie, and then in a more placid manner, added, "And if you're lucky, I'll let you have two slices of bread to dip in your broth."

"Fuck your broth!" Roger snapped. "I don't care if I never eat again, I'm getting the hell out of here." As he ran for the door, his stomach growled, and he was in two minds whether to turn around and apologise, admit he was wrong, and ask if there would be salt and pepper…

He might have done so, had something sharp and hard not thumped into that awkward spot between his shoulder-blades, the place where itches ran amok. "Gnfh!" he said. It wasn't a real word, but it was a solid eleven in scrabble, if you were playing with an amateur. He turned slowly on the spot, reaching back for the blade embedded in his back, knowing he hadn't a cat in Hell's chance of reaching it.

"Look whatcha made me do!" Edie squealed. "You done made me throw a knife at your back!"

"I can…I can see *that*," Roger groaned. Blood drooled from the corner of his mouth. The colour drained from him instantly. Perhaps worst of all, he shit his pantaloons. They say that in those moments before death, one's life flashes before one's eyes; the only thing flashing before Roger Death's eyes was the smell of his own—

"Crap!" said Edie. "Crap and fiddlesticks, I

din't want to 'ave to kill ya."

Roger dropped to his knees, swaying back and forth like a tree in the breeze. "That rhymes," said he.

"*What* does?" Edie frowned.

"Never mind," Roger said, closing his eyes and smacking his lips feverishly together. He glanced at the thing on the table, saw that it was almost the shape of a man, and shook his head. "He's going to…he's going to kill…*again*," he said. He had given up trying to reach the blade jutting from his back, which was as elusive as Lord Lucan, Amelia Earhart, and the clitoris combined.

"*Squeeeeee!*" said the body as it lunged forward into a sitting position. Roger couldn't help but smile at how ridiculous the whole scenario was.

"See you in *Hell*," said the witchdoctor-cum-carpet cleaner. And then he died, and did so in such a dramatic fashion, Edie Travers clapped her approval.

"*Squeeeeee!*" said Larry as he examined the room and tried to figure out what was happening.

"Never you mind '*Squeeeee!*' you idle bastard," Edie said. "There's a pigsty outside wot needs a jolly good mucking out. And when you've done that, I know of two bodies wot need burying. And when you're done with the bodies, I…"

Larry pushed the old bag's voice to the back of his mind as it continued to spout forth orders and menial chores. *Typical,* he thought. *Been dead for fuck knows how long, and now she expects me to dig right in, no warming up, not even a stretch of the old legs.* Now he knew how Sammo Hung felt.

There was something in Larry's right hand. As his senses returned and the nerves knitted back together, he felt it there, enveloped by his gorilla-fist, and when he looked, he saw that it was an axe, and when he realised he was holding an axe, he felt much better, because people with axes are not to be messed with. The same goes for people with guns, hand-grenades, kirpans, light-sabres, Molotov cocktails, machetes, bear-traps, foul-language, religion, dirty syringes, epilepsy, unkempt toenails, STDs, weak bladders, strong bladders, two eyes, four eyes, double-barrelled names, deep trouser pockets, banjos, green teeth, brown pants, boss-eyes, and anyone that tries to push in front of you at a U2 concert (those people have serious issues).

"I'll take *that*, thank you," Edie said, snatching the axe from his languorous grip. "You can have it back when you've peeled the first couple o' layers

LARRY II: THE SQUEEQUEL

off of the toilet bowl."

"*SqueeeeeeeeiiiiiiiiiiIIIIII* haven't even been here making a mess of the place," he said, his voice slightly cracked. "And who the *fuck* is that dead fella?" He pointed to the slumped, motionless body of Roger Death – carpet cleaner by trade, voodoo practitioner when there's not much choice in the matter.

"Why don't you do everything I've asked?" Edie said, "And I'll tell you all about it."

"Sounds like a plan," said Larry, reaching up and fingering the eyeholes of his mask. "Is this thing on me permanently now, like Jennifer Garner's mangled toes, or Megan Fox's clubbed thumbs?"

"I guess it is," Edie said.

And, "Fuck!" said Larry, because no matter how long you're dead for, the best words are always the ones which would make a nun weep.

4
Elm Street (Not that one, but still…)

Amanda Bateman fell out of her bed with a meaty thump. When she came to almost fifteen minutes later, she clambered to her feet and ran through the series of events she had just dreamt about.

Larry Travers back from the dead. Some old bag slurping parsnip soup from an oversized spoon. A dead guy who Amanda recognised as the fella who got the red wine out of her mother's favourite Egyptian rug so many years ago.

Amanda felt sick, for she hadn't thought about the events from the previous summer for a while. It had indeed knocked her bandy. Three mugs of coffee and a half packet of cigarettes later, she picked up the phone and began to punch in a number. It was, after all, the best way to get through to your desired contact.

"Hello?" said a voice on the other end of the line, though it wasn't the voice she'd expected. This voice belonged to a man, or one of those really gruff women that stand around outside office buildings, smoking and discussing their favourite Patrick Swayze movies.

"Erm, I was hoping to speak with Betsy,"

LARRY II: THE SQUEEQUEL

Amanda said. "Betsy Krueger?"

There was a slight pause, just long enough for Amanda to swallow a fourth mug of coffee, and then the voice came back, all apologetic and delicate, as if there was something wrong. "Who might I ask is calling?"

"My name is Amanda Bateman. I'm a friend of Betsy's." That wasn't quite true. They were acquaintances, at best. You could only get so friendly with a person who had decapitated another person, whether they were in the right, or not. "She told me to call this number if I ever needed to talk."

"And you *did*," said the voice. "Good for you, and have a lovely day."

"Wait!" Amanda said.

"What for?"

"I need to talk to Betsy," Amanda said. "It's *extremely* important."

"I'm afraid I have some terrible news for you," said the voice. Bad news was bad, but terrible news, well that could only be… "Betsy died last night in her sleep."

The breath caught in Amanda's throat – it was that horrid morning breath, too, the stuff that tastes like assholes. "There must be some mistake!" she cried.

"Oh, no, she's definitely dead," the voice said. "I'm here now, at her place, and I've seen the body, all bloated and blue and wet."

"I thought you said she died in her sleep?" said Amanda.

"She *did*," said the voice. "She fell asleep in the bathtub. I reckon it was the drowning that killed her."

This was horrible, horrible news. Amanda couldn't believe it, and stood there in a state of shock for several moments while the voice on the other end of the line harked on about rubber ducks and silver pubic hair.

"If it's any consolation," said the voice, "she had an expression on her face that made it look as if she'd died of absolute terror, and not because of the water that had filled her lungs."

How, Amanda thought, could that be considered a consolation? "Terror, you say?" Amanda asked. "What did she look like?"

There was a rustle, and then the man on the other end of the line said, "A bit like that, but without the moustache and ear-hair."

"You're going to have to explain it to me," Amanda said, shaking her head incredulously.

LARRY II: THE SQUEEQUEL

"Explain what she looked like."

"She looked as if she'd seen the Devil," said the man. "And there was a nugget of shit floating about in the tub with her. I reckon that thing was literally scared out of her by someone or some*thing*."

Amanda closed her eyes and took a deep breath. "*Larry*," she said.

"No," said the man. "*Bosher*. I live in the apartment opposite Betsy's. I wouldn't say I knew her that well, but the police have left the door wide open, so I thought I'd pop in and see what all the fuss was about."

Amanda hung up, and as soon as the phone was in its cradle, she broke down in tears. After roughly thirty minutes of sobbing and shaking, and precisely three minutes of blowing snot-bubbles, she managed to pull herself together. She reached for the phone again, punched in a different number, one which she had used plenty of times in the last twelve months.

"Huh-hullo?"

"Freddy," she said, which was perfectly acceptable as that was his name. "He's back. *Larry's* back!"

"Whoa, whoa, calm *down*," Freddy Crowley

said. "Amanda, Larry *died* last year. Betsy Krueger chopped him into little pieces with his own fucking axe."

"Betsy's *dead!*" Amanda screeched.

"What? How did she—"

"In her sleep, kind of," Amanda said, for she wasn't sure what had happened there. "You have to listen to me, Freddy. I *saw* him. I saw *Larry*, and he was up and about, *squeeeing* and smelling of bacon, just like he was last summer."

"When did you see him?" Freddy suddenly sounded interested. "Where *was* this?"

"Last night," Amanda said. "He was in my dream, and he'd just killed this great carpet-cleaner guy my family used—"

"Did you say that you *dreamt* this?" Freddy said. "And you're calling me, why?"

"Look, this isn't a coincidence," Amanda said. "I feel different. It's as if Larry's resurrection has stirred something in me." Like a fart, she thought, but less bubbly.

"Okay, I'm going to hang up now, and I want you to go back to bed, okay?"

"I don't need *sleep*," Amanda said. "I need you to listen to me. We knew this day would come, didn't we? We were speaking about it only last week."

"Sequel day," Freddy muttered. "But that was just *talk*, wasn't it. I mean, did you really think it was possible?"

"Chopping Larry into pieces was never going to do the trick," Amanda said.

"We set fire to him, as well," Freddy reminded her. "I mean, surely *that* should have been enough?"

"You would have *thought* so," said Amanda. "But we've both watched enough horror movies to know that the villain is practically invincible. The best we can hope for is that this whole thing doesn't develop into a franchise." Amanda could already picture it. Pigface adorning cups, jigsaw-puzzles, mouse-mats, biros, cushions, shower-curtains, stationary, baseball caps, socks, disposable lighters, Zippo lighters, USB sticks, and so on, and so forth.

"I wouldn't mind being in the third one, though," Freddy said. "3D is the shizzle."

"I don't think you're taking this seriously," Amanda said.

"You're right," replied Freddy. In fact, he wasn't taking it seriously to the point that he had drawn several tiny cocks on the notepad beside the telephone. Good cocks they were, too. He was very proud of them.

"So what are we going to do about it?" Amanda said. Her notepad was blank, for she wasn't equipped with enough knowledge of the male genitalia to have a go at doodling one.

"Well," Freddy said, sketching a line of tattie water from one of the cocks – an integral part of the design, and something he'd picked up in school. "If he's back, I would suggest we stay the hell away from Camp Diamond Creek and hope he doesn't learn to drive."

"That's it, is it?" Amanda said, scribbling out her useless attempt at a vagina. "That's your plan?"

Freddy sighed. "My plan was to take a shower, eat last night's leftover pizza, and head over to the arcade where I was going to spend the rest of the day feeding quarters into this new game they've got there. It's like Pac-Man, but instead of ghosts chasing you, it's toothbrushes."

"Plaque-Man?" Amanda said.

"Face Invaders."

"Look, we need to do something about this. We need to make sure he doesn't kill again. He took all of our friends from us, remember?"

Freddy finished scribbling pubes and dropped

his pencil. "Of course I remember. How could I forget? There was the geeky one, the black one, that dumb girly one who was lucky to make it as far as she did, in my honest opinion."

"Oh my God, you've forgotten their names! Freddy…"

"Crowley," he said.

"Freddy Crowley, you should be ashamed of yourself."

"I am," he said. "All the time, actually, but I don't see what that has to do with our little predicament."

"He's going to come for us," Amanda said, though how she knew that, she wasn't sure. "He isn't going to stop until he's rammed his axe so far up our asses that we're shitting splinters for a month."

"We could always go to the hospital to get it re—"

"It was a figure of speech, dickwad." Amanda was growing increasingly frustrated; she'd taken to drawing Pigface on her notepad, a knife jutting from the top of his head. It looked nothing like him, and the knife (banana?) was questionable, but she knew what it was meant to be. "I'm not going to stand by and watch as more innocent people are butchered by that bastard."

"And the best way to *not* see any of that butchering going on," Freddy said, "is to steer well clear of Camp Diamond Creek. How many times do I have to tell you? For a final girl, you really are stubborn."

Before Amanda knew what she was doing, she'd hung up the phone. The colour she had turned – ripe eggplant, if you were to buy it in a tin from a hardware store – revealed only a fraction of the anger she felt in that moment.

Deep breath… deep breath… calm down…

"I'll show you final girl," she said, holding the notepad up so that she was face-to-face with her enemy, Banana-Head Wild Boar. "You're going to wish you'd stayed dead, you sonofabitch." And with that she tore the page from the notepad, crumpled it up into a little ball – after she'd wiped her ass with it – and tossed it in the waste-paper basket next to the phone table, where it would eventually rot away to nothing.

LARRY II: THE SQUEEQUEL

5
The Travers Cabin

Edie had just finished lopping the good meat off the sheriff and the carpet-cleaner – waste not, want not – and was about to bury what was left of them when Larry came a-rushing out the back door, squee-ing excitedly, his axe in one hand and a copy of *Reader's Digest* in the other.

Edie almost had a heart-attack, for she was at the right age for suchlike. "Can you not do that!" she gasped, swallowing bile and doubling over. "I'm still comin' to terms with the fact you 'ave to keep that bleedin' thing on all the time now." She motioned to the mask which was now, apparently, his permanent face.

Don't listen to her, said the mask, in its usual italicised dialect. *She'll be gone soon, if I have anything to do with it. In fact, why don't you pop back inside and come out again, only this time without your clothes on?*

"She's *alive*!" Larry said, breathlessly.

"Who?" Edie picked up her shovel and continued digging. "The Queen of England? Zsa Zsa Gabor? Betty 'The Immortal' White?"

"That bitch from last year!" Larry said. "The one that got away."

"I thought there were *two* that got away," said Edie, dragging a mutilated body across the glade. "*Three* if you count the one that got away in 1978. Really, Larry," – she kicked the corpse into its respective hole and lit a roll-yer-own – "I'm surprised you're as famous as you are, what with all the one's that got away."

Larry pointed at the cabin. "I was in there," he said, "taking a shit and reading about dandruff remedies, when all of a sudden I saw her."

"What's she doin' in our fucking bathroom?" Edie said, reaching for the shovel. "I'll donk her over the 'ead with this if I 'ave to. Don't tell me, you let her get away. Seems to be the order of the day around here."

"No, I saw her in my *head*," Larry said, tapping at his temple with the butt of his axe.

Edie regarded her son the same way one might regard a mentally-handicapped meerkat or a one-legged donkey. *The lights are on*, she thought, *but the bastard's gone on holiday…*

"I'd just crimped off a second wave of nuggets when it hit me," Larry continued. "She was just standing there, looking at some picture of a wild boar with a banana sticking out the top of its head."

LARRY II: THE SQUEEQUEL

Edie tilted her head to the side, now regarding him in the same way she would a piece of roadkill, or the Kardashian tribe.

"She's still out there, Ma, and do you know what she's doing?"

"Drawing pictures of wild boar with bananas sticking out of their 'eads, by the sounds of it."

"She's *mocking* me!" There, he'd said it. "She's out there somewhere, and she's…she's taking the *piss* out of me."

Edie snorted. "Larry, Larry, Larry." It was a good job he wasn't Candyman, or she'd be pulling a hook out of her va-jay-jay by now. "All of that silliness, it's in the past now. I don't know why you wanna go dredging it all up again."

See, I told you she'd say that, the mask whispered. *I say we just chop her head off and bury her with those two schmucks.*

"She got away," Edie continued. "Because she's the final girl, and that's what they're there for."

Seriously, we could clobber her right now and no-one would give a shit…

"I have to go after her," said Larry. "I can't just sit around here while she's out there, taking the proverbial and creating terrible artwork." He swung the axe in a wide arc through the air. It *whooshed*, as was its wont, before landing in a thicket with his arm still attached. There was a moment's silence, as one might expect when something so unexpected happens.

"Bloody hell!" Edie said. "You've only gone and thrown your arm off." She flicked her cigarette into the open grave and dropped the shovel. "Come on. Inside. And you'd better 'ope I can remember where I put my fuckin' sewing-kit."

*

Larry watched as she threaded the needle in and out of his shoulder, drawing the arm back into its rightful place. The smell was awful – like an abattoir, but without all the smoking middle-aged men comparing chauvinistic jokes. Larry understood why his ma had insisted upon wearing a heavy-duty dust-mask.

Go on, tell her, said the mask. *And don't take no for an answer, you hear me?*

"I'm still going, Ma," Larry said.

"No," said Edie.

Beneath the mask Larry scrunched his face up, for he hated going against her wishes, despite how much he loathed her. At the end of the day she had raised him, reared him from the shy little urchin he'd been to the much-feared slasher he was

LARRY II: THE SQUEEQUEL

today. If that wasn't the sign of good parenting, Larry didn't know what was.

"We have a *connection* now," he went on. "Some sort of psychic bond."

"What, like Penn and Teller?"

"Yeah, like *NO*, nothing like Penn and Teller," he said. "Who the fuck are Penn and Teller?"

"Couple of wankers from Vegas," Edie said. "Now hold still, otherwise you'll be wearing your arm on your earlobe."

Larry winced as the needle hooked deep into his flesh before emerging once again, covered in what looked like bacon, which kind of made sense.

Go on, urged the mask. *Honestly, am I the only one around here with a pair?*

"If I can see what she's doing," Larry pressed on, reluctantly, "then there's a damn good chance she can see what I'm doing."

"Well you'd better stop masturbating in the pigsty then, hadn't you," Edie said, forcing the needle deep into his skin once again.

"*Ouch!*" and, "How do you know what I do in the pigsty?" He should have been embarrassed, but he and his mother were close enough to discuss such taboo subjects. Besides, he knew that she flicked her bean to old photographs of Cary

Grant. In fact, she had a whole heap of them in her second drawer down. Larry had stumbled upon them when he had been searching for something sexy to try on.

"I ain't stupid," Edie said, winking and running her black tongue across her sole tooth. "And I ain't dumb enough to believe that you've been applying cream to Wilbur's back because of some Mad Pig's Disease."

Wilbur, Larry thought, must have grassed him up. "Anyway, stop trying to change the subject, Ma. This is hard enough as it is, without you bringing up my tugging habits. I'm trying to tell you that I'm offski. Gone like the wind. Off to greener pastures, or in this case Haddon."

"*Haddon?*" Edie frowned. "Why would you wanna go to *Haddon?* Even the people what live there don't want to go to *Haddon*. There's nothing there for you, Larry. Nothing but disappointment and scorn, and I can give you loads of that without you even 'aving to leave the cabin. At least 'ere you get three square meals a day, providin' you don't mind chowing down on carpet-cleaner."

Don't take no for an answer, the voice of the mask reminded him.

"I won't take no for answer," Larry said.

LARRY II: THE SQUEEQUEL

"What about 'definitely not'?"

Larry shook his head. "That's pretty much the same thing."

"On no account?"

"Now you're just poshing it up," said Larry, staring down at the huge black scar he now wore at the top of his arm. "Are we done here? I've got some packing to do."

Just then, and all of a sudden, Edie stood up and threw herself backwards. Her head missed the corner of the table by no more than an inch, and she landed in a heap on the floorboards. "Oh! Whoooooaaaaahhhh!" she wailed. "I think I's 'aving dizzy spells. Oh, 'ere comes another one." She rolled along the cabin floor, her bones rattling against the wood. It sounded like someone was trying to drag a bag of spanners up an uncarpeted set of stairs. When she came to a stop, she cried, "Ya wanna leave you're ol' ma like this? Just leave me 'ere to rot while you go off gallivanting to Haddon?" She raised a hand to her head. "Fuck, I think I'm dyin' Larry," she said. "I'm dyin' an' you won't be 'ere to see it."

Don't listen to her, the mask said. *She'll see a hundred, make no mistake about it.*

"Ma, stop this nonsense," Larry said, easing his

weary bones up from the chair. "I won't be gone long. I just need to find the final girl, decapitate her, and Bob's your mother's brother, I'll be back before your next bath." That gave him at least six weeks if the shit hit the fan, which it most probably would.

Sensing his determination, Edie Travers peeled her desiccated body up from the floorboards and dusted herself down. "Haddon's not the place for a Pigface like you," she said, for she wasn't quite ready to give up the ghost just yet. "The city's 'orrible. There are wimmin what sell their bodies for sex and fellas on every corner forcing crack cocaine into your 'ands."

I thought she was trying to talk us out of it, said the mask.

"You ain't ever left these woods, Larry. You don't know what 'orrors are lurkin' in Haddon." She moved slowly across the room, stared out through the cabin window, or would have done if the thing hadn't been boarded up twenty-five years ago. "I went there once," she said. "Only for a packet of jerky, but I was only there five minutes before a bunch of reprobates took me into an alley and gave me a jolly good buggerin'."

Larry was gobsmacked. "Oh, Ma. That's

awful." And it *was* awful. Mainly for the reprobates that did the buggerin'.

"Yeah, I've never mentioned it before," she went on. "But now seems the right time. Larry, I don't want *you* getting buggered in an alleyway by five handsome guys who paid up front, despite you telling them that it was on the house."

Larry frowned.

"I don't want you coming back here with PTSD, waking up in the middle of the night on a sodden pillow, limping because your ass has been fubar-ed." She sighed and began to roll a cigarette. Larry took that as a sign that she'd finished her sad story-cum-fond remembrance.

"I'm not being funny, Ma, but I doubt whether five handsome guys with cash on the hip are gonna wanna bugger a serial-killing porcine-faced growler like me in a dark alleyway."

"It wasn't a *dark* alleyway," Edie said, lighting her cigarette. "This was broad daylight. There were kids there. One of them was taking pictures."

"My point is," Larry said, about to make his point, "I can look after myself. I've butchered more people than Kim Jong Un. I've slashed my way through more virgins than Russell Brand. I've—"

"I get the picture," Edie said. "And it sounds like nothing I say is goin' to make you change your mind. Just don't come cryin' to me when it all goes tits up, *nosiree*."

Beneath the mask that was now a permanent fixture upon his heavily-disfigured bonce, Larry's lips curled up a little. He'd done it. He had actually stood up to her and won. He'd never felt so pleased with himself in all his life (though, he was practically dead now, so he wasn't even sure if it counted).

"Just promise me one thing," Edie said, taking a lung-busting drag on her roll-yer-own.

"What? *Anything*, you name it."

"If you see five handsome guys carrying a packet of out-of-date jerky, let 'em know where I am."

LARRY II: THE SQUEEQUEL

6
Haddon Airport – Terminal Two (For Posh People)

Sam Treat descended the steps of her private jet and took in a huge lungful of Haddon air. When she'd stopped spluttering almost three whole minutes later, she turned to her assistant and said, "Make a note. One second breaths maximum," and her personal assistant, Martha Blankenship, flipped open a notepad and did just as Sam Treat told her to.

Sam Treat was beautiful. Voted number 49 in *Heat Magazine's World's Hottest Women Feature 2015* (only 48 places behind Megan Fox, 26 places behind Michelle Obama, and one place behind Camilla Parker-Bowles), she had certainly been blessed in the looks department. Her long blonde hair cascaded down over her flawless shoulders; her large green eyes looked as if they had been drawn on by a Japanese cartoonist; her breasts were both the same size and her vagina went the right way, which was a cheeky bonus for anyone lucky enough to get a sniff of it. She was a remarkably fanciable human being.

As is the case with most people of a

prepossessing and vain nature, she was also a prize cunt, or as her personal assistant Martha Blankenship liked to call her, Lady Cunt-Cunt.

Martha Blankenship, you see, was at the other end of the attractiveness spectrum (not to be confused with the ZX Spectrum). She had not been blessed with the looks of her charge. In fact, she had been royally buggered – though not in a dark alleyway – by the God of Good Looks, and so walked around with her jowls flapping and her eyes overlapping like something that had been tampered with by aliens, only for them to decide it was far too tricky and that the best thing to do was to return her to earth, mangled face or not. Still, she made do with what she had, which was not much since Lady Cunt-Cunt was also something of a miser. Martha Blankenship hadn't seen a payslip for almost six months, and whenever she mentioned it, Sam Treat threatened to replace her with one of those tiny handbag dogs. Since she couldn't afford to lose her seemingly non-paying job, Martha would back down, but she was as shrewd as she was ugly, oh yes, mark my words. Martha Blankenship had been stealing diamonds from Lady Cunt-Cunt for the last three months. First set of drawers in the master bedroom, second drawer down, behind the pink furry handcuffs and do-it-yourself Vajazzle set, was a black satin bag, and in that bag were hundreds and hundreds of tiny diamonds. So many diamonds were there that Martha had helped herself to at least twenty of the little blighters. It would be ruder not to help herself, or so she believed.

"So this is Haddon," Sam said, walking across the airport tarmac as if she was back on the Versace catwalk.

"That's what the sign says," Martha replied, motioning to the huge placard hanging over the terminal entrance. "If you wanted to go somewhere else, we could always hop back on the jet."

"What, and miss the party of the century?" Sam paused in front of a row of over-excited photographers. It was as if they had never seen such beauty before. Coming from Haddon, there was a good chance that they hadn't.

"This way, Sam!" *Snap!*

"Over here, Miss Treat!" *Snap!*

"Can somebody move that ugly boiler out of the shot, please!" *Snap!*

"Do you have any idea how much tickets are for Harry Hunter's party? Do you have any idea who's going to be there?" Sam spun around so the paparazzi could get a good view of her jacksie. And a jolly fine Jacksie it was, too. One of the photographers fell to his knees, gasping and clutching his chest. It would be three hours before anyone noticed him lying dead on the runway.

"I've heard about Harry Hunter and his parties," Martha said. "Is it true he has eight wives?"

"*Seven*," Sam said, playing up to the press, which was just what they wanted for their low-rent tabloids and filth mags. "One of them fell out of a seventh-storey window up at his mansion last week. Rumour has it that he was doing her so hard from behind, he shot her across the room and over the handrail."

"Isn't that murder?" Martha asked.

"Depends how you look at it."

"I'm looking at it from the blood-spattered ground below the seventh-storey window."

"Well if you look at it like that—"

"Car for Miss Treat!" bellowed a portly looking fellow from the terminal doors.

"Ah, that's us!" Sam said. "Come on, Martha. We've only got twenty-four hours to prepare for this party." She looked her assistant up and down, and then up again, just in case she'd made some terrible mistake. "We'll just concentrate on making me look super, ja?"

"Ja," said Martha, which was amazing, really, as she hadn't taken an Afrikaans lesson in her entire life.

7
Armand's Arcade – Haddon

"And she reckons his Pigface fucker's going to come *here*? To *Haddon*?" Richard Goodnight said, hammering at the joystick and buttons in front of him as if it had slept with his mother and then shared the experience to Instagram.

Freddy, leaning against the machine – *Sonic the Little Spiky Blue Bastard III* – shrugged. "That's what she thinks," he said.

"And you don't?" said Richard, followed by, "Agh, fuck you, you little spiky blue bastard!"

"I don't know what's wrong with her," Freddy said. "I mean, what happened to us up there was terrible. Some real fucked up shit. It was like the first part in some terrible franchise, you know?"

"Did it ever feel," Richard said, feeding more coins into the machine, "that there would be an inevitable sequel? You know what I'm talking about. Like, is there any chance that this Pigface fucker didn't die – like *really* die?"

Freddy shook his head in the negative; any other way would have been a nod. "Pretty sure we saw his arms and legs come off," he said. "And then the place went up quicker than Paul

LARRY II: THE SQUEEQUEL

Gascoigne at a family barbecue. I'd say it would take some sort of miracle to bring him back."

"Or voodoo," Richard said. He head-butted the screen in frustration. "You little spiky blue *motherfucker!*" He fed more coins into the machine. "Seriously, you might want to look into that. Those witchcrafty types are complete nutters. A mate of mine…well, I say mate, but he's more of a friend of a…well, I say friend of a—"

"Skip to the end."

"Anyway, this complete stranger, he went to this island village to look for this missing girl, right? Ended up on fire in a giant man of wicker."

"Isn't that the plot of *The Wicker Man*?"

"*Might* be," Richard said, thoughtful stroking the tuft of fluff that he hoped would one day blossom into a full beard. "My point is, whatever you do, never go to Scotland."

Freddy sighed and tried to imagine what it would be like to have intelligent friends. "So you think Amanda might be right?" he said. "She seemed pretty fucking certain about it."

"Women are like *guns*, man," Richard said, turning from Sonic the Little Spiky Blue Bastard III and scanning the arcade for his next piece of action.

"Quick to fire *off?*" Freddy ventured, though he should have known better.

"You keep one around long enough, you're gonna wanna shoot it." And with that little nugget of misogyny, Richard Goodnight stalked across the room to the newest machine. Freddy reluctantly followed. A pair of guns were pointed at the screen, and Richard latched onto the one on the left. "Feel free to join in," he said, motioning to the second gun.

"*Anders Breivik's Day Off?*" Freddy said, pointing to the already-peeling vinyl at the top of the machine. "That's a bit close to the fucking knuckle, ain't it?"

Richard chuckled. He was a cunt like that. "Yeah, Armand said he got it dirt cheap."

"Not surprised," Freddy said, before taking hold of the second gun. "Back to my problem—"

"Can't we just shoot some Norse kids and have a bit of peace and quiet?" Richard said, clearly annoyed. "Pigface is *dead*! You said you saw him, lying there in six pieces! I ain't no doctor, but I reckon he was past the point of resuscitation!"

"Fine, fine!" Freddy said, lining up a shot. He took it and missed, though he was secretly glad. There was something intrinsically wrong about

LARRY II: THE SQUEEQUEL

unloading on a bunch of schoolkids, but you try telling that to Rolf Harris…

After Richard's little outburst, Freddy found it difficult to concentrate on anything. When Armand threw them both out a little over an hour later – something about getting ketchup all over his joysticks – he decided to call Amanda. Smooth things over. Tell her he was sorry, and that there was a chance she was right about this.

If Pigface *was* back, Freddy damn well wanted the final girl on his side. Much less chance of having his bollocks hacked off with a rusty axe.

8
Elm Street (Still not that one)

Amanda stood over the bed, staring down at the vast array of objects she had collected from around the apartment. With her mother out of town for the foreseeable future – some sex-toy conference on the other side of the country; *DildoFest 2015*, or something – Amanda knew she had time on her side. Time to put these potential weapons back where she found them.

"Okay," she said, picking up a cheese-grater and tossing it across the room. She wanted to *kill* the fucker, not take the hard-skin off his heels. "Let's see what we've got."

What she had, she realised after thirty seconds of rummaging, was a whole lot of nothing. Any knives she had previously thought useful were about as blunt as a bag of wet mice. At least she could hit the psycho over the head with a bag of wet mice; she didn't trust these knives to butter a piece of toast without buckling under the pressure.

A hammer! She picked it up, swung it in a wide arc, and watched in dismay as its head flew off and smashed into her dressing-table mirror. Once the glass had settled, she said, "Fuck," and dropped what was now essentially a small wooden hitting-stick onto the floor.

A Swiss Army knife was next to disappoint. Its knife had been snapped off about halfway up the blade, and the miniature saw was missing more teeth than the entire cast of *Duck Dynasty* combined. There was a decent flat-headed screwdriver, but again, she wanted to kill the bastard, not knock him up an Ikea wardrobe.

After five minutes of weapon-inspection, she came to the conclusion that she had no weapons. She would have to fend Pigface off with strong language and harsh stares.

Just then, as it was wont to do when one least expected it, the phone rang. Amanda left the pile of useless implements on the bed and went to answer it.

"Amanda!" Freddy's voice said before she'd even picked up. Of course, she didn't hear him say her name, for she hadn't picked up yet.

"Hello?" Amanda said, finally picking up after not picking up a moment ago.

"You might be right," Freddy said. "I hate to admit it, but you might be right."

"Right about what?" Amanda said, picking up the pen she had been doodling with earlier and wielding it like a sword.

"About *Pigface*," Freddy said. "About him coming back from the dead."

"What made you change your mind?" She couldn't help feeling a little smug. Of course she was right. She was the final girl. The final girl is always right. Until they get there head smashed off with a sledgehammer.

"I was at the arcade with Rich," said Freddy. "He said something about voodoo, about how you shouldn't trust anyone that wears robes and talks in tongues."

"What about the Pope?" asked Amanda.

"No, I didn't see *him* at the arcade. Anyway, my point is that, if what you're saying is true, that we're about to come face-to-face with that bacon-faced bastard once again, we need to prepare."

"I was just doing—" Amanda trailed off as dizziness washed over her. She had to grasp onto the telephone table to prevent herself from toppling backwards. She hadn't felt this woozy since the first time she fingered herself.

"Amanda? Amanda? You still there?"

The truth of the matter was, she *wasn't* there. Well, of course she was still *bodily* there. If she *wasn't*, then things had really taken a turn for the worse. If you had been there in her hallway, you would have seen her, swaying slowly back and forth, drooling slightly, eyes staring off into the middle-distance, as if she was trying to remember something just out of reach. And though she was still there, phone to her ear, dribble on her chin, piss running down her ankles, her mind was somewhere else entirely.

Somewhere it didn't want to be.

*

"Ma, have you seen my axe-sharpener?"

"What does it look like?" came the reply.

"It looks like something you could sharpen an axe with."

"Does it look like a whetstone?"

"Kind of, but it's shaped like a hockey puck."

"Oh! A hockey-puck shaped whetstone?"

"Yeah, that's it."

"No, I haven't seen it."

"Oh, for fuck's sake." Gigantic arthritis-riddled hands reached across and picked up an axe. The axe went into a suitcase which appeared to be held together with duct tape. Already in the suitcase were several large knives, a length of rope, a map of Haddon (outdated by about twenty years, but a map, nonetheless), a copy of 60+ Sluts Magazine, a bloody apron, and a scented candle. To an outside viewer, if

indeed there was one, the scented candle might have come across as overkill.

"Please believe me when I saaaaay," sang Larry. "This is how it has to end. This is easy on us all, well easier than other waaaays." Into the case went a packet of extra-strong mints — because nothing said 'Dead Slasher' more than halitosis — and a roll of toilet-paper — because nothing said 'Dead Slasher' more than a dirty asshole, except maybe halitosis.

"You're really doing this?" a voice from behind asked. Edie Travers, standing in the doorway, looked to be on the verge of a mental breakdown. She hadn't had one for a while, and so it was long overdue, and Larry's insistence upon leaving her to her own devices — no amount of Cary Grant photos would get her through this — was just the kind of thing to push her over the edge.

"We already talked about this, Ma," Larry said, slamming the lid of his suitcase shut and fastening it with a padlock. The fact that a sudden gust of wind would rip the whole thing to bits was neither here nor there. "I've got to finish her. The final girl must die. That's how this works."

"I thought the final girl lived?" said Edie, scratching her beard with confusion.

"In part one," Larry said. "I'm thinking that me dying signalled the end of that, and me coming back meant

LARRY II: THE SQUEEQUEL

the start of part two. Is there any chance this might be a trilogy? Only I've always fancied being in 3D."

"Let's hope not," said Edie. "Look, son, you've made your point. Why don't you unpack your case and come and sit down in the dark with absolutely nothing to do but twiddle your thumbs? Huh? You're pushing seventy, Larry. You shouldn't be off killing people; you should be relaxing, sucking wine-gums, foraging in your ears for something to play with."

"No," Larry said, picking up the suitcase. "I'm off to Haddon, and nothing you say is going to change my mind."

"Bollocks," said Edie.

*

When Amanda came to, she glanced around the hallway as if she had been mysteriously teleported there. Freddy's panicked voice was yelling into her ear. "Hello! Amanda! Hello! For fuck's sa—"

"He's coming," Amanda said. "He's coming, Freddy, and he's packed a suitcase."

"Oh," went Freddy.

"Oh," added Amanda.

And outside, millions of other people went *Oh!* at the exact same time, though that was just synchronicity and had nothing at all to do with Larry Travers, or the fact that he'd packed a suitcase.

9
Haddon City Centre

Johnnie Ketchum had been the mayor of Haddon for almost a year, and in that year he had opened more than fifty stores, three museums, a visitors' centre, half-a-dozen taxi-ranks, fifteen breweries, and the *Phat Phuc Noodle Bar* over on Green Street. He estimated that he'd spent more than twenty-two entire days, standing next to a ribbon with a pair of scissors in his hand, which is where we now find him, looking moderately dejected and wondering what would happen if he was to suddenly plunge the scissors into his own eye-socket, apart from the bleeding obvious.

"It gives me great pleasure," he lied, "to be here today," the lie went on, "opening this wonderful new tanning salon," *scissors in eye, scissors in eye*, his brain suggested. To his right, three bright orange ladies wearing luminous orange t-shirts and appallingly short orange skirts, applauded as if it was the first time they had ever heard a human speak. "Yes, indeed," Johnnie said, before waiting for them to stop it.

There was a decent crowd gathered around the new tanning salon – *Tan Yo Hide*, for anyone that might have been wondering – which was remarkable, really, since the sun offered almost the exact same service, free of charge. People, Johnnie thought, had no patience any more. They couldn't be bothered with all that sitting on the beach malarkey, where they risked sand-chafe and crab-bites and shark-attacks and gratuitous nudity courtesy of some shrivelled-up old crone whose breasts hung like Dachshund ears. People wanted to wake up pastier than Casper on a Saturday morning and be walking around illuminating their entire neighbourhoods by lunchtime. Skin cancer? Ah, that's a small price to pay for the ability to render oneself an oompa loompa.

"It was only last month," Johnnie continued, "that I lay in bed, thinking—"

"*Wanking!*" someone from the crowd shouted.

"*Thinking!*" Johnnie yelled back. "Thinking that what this city needed was yet another tanning salon." He turned to the orange women, who regarded him warily, now, as if they were afraid of what he might say next. "And here you are, the answer to my prayers." His knuckles were white from squeezing the scissors too hard." He stepped up to the ribbon, allowed those with cameras to, for whatever strange reason, capture the moment forever, and then snipped it, all the time smiling like a dog with a bout of wind.

The orange women all wanted a kiss from him – of *course* they fucking well did – and Johnnie spent the rest of the afternoon handing out 2for1 vouchers, just in case gravy-browning wasn't dark enough for you.

I'd do anything for a bit of action, Johnnie thought, passing vouchers to five handsome men sharing a packet of past-its-best jerky. *Anything.*

*

Across the city, where a new tanning salon would be popping up in just a few weeks' time, was an alleyway. This wasn't uncommon, of course; most cities have alleyways. Where else would the junkies dispose of their needles if they didn't? This particular alleyway was slightly different to all the others, however, inasmuch as it was home to one of Hollywood's forgotten heroes.

The woman walking through said alleyway had no idea that she was being watched. It was, after all, broad daylight, and rapists, like bats and Lindsay Lohan, only operated at night, or so she thought.

A wolf-whistle told her otherwise.

Coming to a stop in the middle of the alleyway,

LARRY II: THE SQUEEQUEL

equidistant to the safety offered by the busier roads at either end, a horrible noise ripped through her. After apologising profusely, she said, "Who's there?", which was an absolutely stupid thing to say.

"Just us, *chick-a-chick-a*," came the reply. The woman spun to find her escape obstructed by a trio of punks. Brightly-coloured Mohawks, pierced noses and ears, and more dangling chains than at a *Hellraiser* reunion party, these were proper punks, and make no mistake about it. After swallowing her heart back down, the woman turned and—

"For *fuck's* sake!" she gasped as her eyes fell upon even more punks. She was the filling in a punk sandwich. Now she knew how groupies felt backstage at a Stiff Little Fingers concert. She had to think fast, and think fast she did. "I've got AIDS!" she said.

"Ain't we all, love?" asked the punk at the front of the second wave. "Jeb here was one of the first in the country, weren't you Jeb?"

An old punk with turquoise hair and a bone through his nose said, "Caught it off a monkey. Passed it on to Michael Stipe."

The woman's heart was racing, for she knew she was in a spot of bother. "Just let me go," she said. "I won't tell the cops nothing."

"You won't tell 'em nothing, anyway," said the leader. "Now if you'd just be a good girl and take your knickers off, that would—" He was about to say 'that would be spiffing' when something, moving quicker than the eye could see, rushed across from the left of the alleyway and knocked three of his teeth out before disappearing again. The punk just stood there, blood drooling from his lips, a look of exquisite confusion upon his weather-beaten phizog.

The other punks began to laugh. One of them bent, picked up a tooth, and handed it to his leader. "Bloody hell, Zip, how fast were you talking?"

Zip scanned the alleyway. "Something just…something just knocked mah teef out and split mah lip," he said.

"I didn't see anythin'," said Jeb, but that might have been his AIDS playing up.

"Me neither," said a third punk. All six of Zip's comrades denied seeing anything.

"You!" said Zip, marching up to the woman, who was just as shocked by this strange turn of events as the punks. "What did you just do to me?"

"I didn't do *anything!*" the woman gasped.

"You bloody well did," Zip said, fingering his

LARRY II: THE SQUEEQUEL

split lip and pushing a bloody digit toward her as proof. "You're like that Carrie girl, ain'tcha? That Carrie girl from that film? For fuck's sake, what's that film called, the on with that Carrie girl in it?"

"*Star Wars*?" Jeb ventured.

"I didn't do *anything*!" the woman reiterated.

Suddenly, something whooshed through the alleyway. Blurred limbs and cracked skulls were all that the woman saw. It was more than those with the cracked skulls saw, though, as they hit the concrete and began the relatively slow process of bleeding to death.

Zip glanced around at the six punks, who were the ones doing the aforementioned bleeding out. He took a step back, away from the fallen body of Jeb. You didn't have to roger a monkey to get AIDS, not in this day and age.

Turning back to the woman, he looked terrified. "Please! I'm sorry! Don't hurt me!" he begged. "We wasn't gonna do anything to hurt you!"

"You bloody well were!" said the woman, who, for the first time and somewhat confusingly, had the upper hand. "You were going to *rape* me."

Zip looked offended. "No we *weren't*," he said.

"You were. You told me to take my knickers

off!"

Zip pulled a handful of knickers from his leather jacket. "We're the Haddon Halleyway Hunderwear Hooligans!" he cried. "We just pinch peoples' underwear and run about the place, swinging them around our heads and singing the greatest hits of The Clash."

"Oh," said the woman. In Haddon, three other people said *Oh!*, which just went to show that synchronicity worked just as well on a small scale.

"Look what you've done to my gang!" Zip said, motioning to the bloodied bodies carpeting the alleyway. "I'll have to start over from scratch now. Punks are like Pokémon. Rare as rocking-horse shit. You've probably set me back t—"

The blur appeared once again, bolted across the concrete, and picked Zip up by the throat. The woman saw now that the mysterious figure was hooded, though not in a yobbish way. He was, in fact, dressed like a ninja, if ninjas had old pizza-boxes stuck to their plimsoles. His face was concealed by a dark mask – the woman could just about make out a pair of steely eyes.

"Gnph!" Zip said, which was far more than his cohorts had been afforded. "Ach!" Which was amazing, really, as he'd never taken a Scottish class

LARRY II: THE SQUEEQUEL

in his entire life.

With a flick of the wrist, the vagabond ninja snapped Zip's neck, and the old punk dropped to the floor with a meaty thud.

After a few seconds, and realising that the ninja was in no rush to piss off, the woman said: "Who *are* you?" in that way they do in those films with the people, and stuff, with the heroes, and whatnot.

The ninja reached up, removed the hood, then peeled the face-mask away to reveal…

"Julia *Roberts!*" the woman gasped. "What happened to your hair?"

"Actually," the vagabond ninja said, "I'm Eric Roberts. You might have seen me in such action classics as *Best of the Best, Best of the Best II*, and my personal favourite, *Love, Honour & Obey: The Last Mafia Marriage.*"

"Were you in *Mystic Pizza?*" asked the woman.

"No, that was Julia."

"*Steel Magnolias?*"

"Julia."

"*Ocean's Eleven*. Come on, you must have been in that one. *Everyone* was in that one."

"I wasn't," Eric Roberts said. "But Julia was. Look, do I get a thank you, or something, for saving your life?"

"Hardly save my life," said the woman. "They were only going to pinch my knickers."

"*Were* they?" said Eric. "Oh, then I fear I may have overdone it on the old punishment front."

"I fear so, too," said the woman. "Anyway, look, it's been lovely meeting you. Give my love to Julia when you next see her." At that, and with the woman disappearing into the distance as quick as you like, Eric Roberts' face crumpled up as if he'd bitten down an a lemon.

"*Fuck* Julia," he muttered, kicking one of the fallen punks in the face. The punk groaned and spat out blood and teeth. "Fucking princess, getting all the good jobs…got some fucking stories about Julia fucking Roberts…played with herself while her teddy watched…shit the bath when she was thirteen…

LARRY II: THE SQUEEQUEL

10
Camp Diamond Creek

Larry waited until nightfall before making his way through the woods, down past the used condom, right at the frog skeleton, left at the tree with the rudimentary penis carved into it, and onto the road at the bottom of the hill. By the time he arrived at the road, he was absolutely shattered, once again a reminder that he wasn't as young as he used to be. "Fuck!" he said, for he'd forgotten to pack his incontinence pants. He glanced back the hill and, for a moment, considered heading back to the cabin to fetch them.

I wouldn't, said the mask. *I can hear your heartbeat. You're just going to have to shit yourself.*

The mask, as was usually the case, was right. If he was lucky he'd make it halfway before succumbing to a coronary. Shitting himself seemed like the safer option.

Hold your thumb out, the mask said.

"Why?" Larry was confused. He imagined that the next few days would be filled with such confusion. Not to mention lots of frowning, several bouts of shrugging, a plethora of questions, and an almost infinite supply of 'what the fuck?s'.

How else do you expect to thumb a ride? said the mask. *That's why it's called thumbing a ride. It's not called 'nonchalantly standing with your hands in your pockets' a ride.*

"It should be," said Larry. "My hands are fucking freezing." Reluctantly, he slipped his left hand from the warmth of its pocket and held it out, thumb extended.

Other way, said the mask. *People will think your criticizing their driving skills.*

Larry turned his hand so that the thumb pointed upward. "Now what?"

Now we wait, said the mask. *For a ridiculous amount of time, by the looks of it. Seriously, you couldn't find a busier road than this? Mars sees more traffic than this road. The last time a car came along here, Henry Ford was driving the fucker.*

"This is the only road I *know*," Larry said. "I'm sure someone will be along in a bit."

Yeah, if they're lost, said the mask. *This road has seen less action than Stephen Hawking.*

"Are you going to be like this the entire time?" Larry said. "Because I'll leave you…" He trailed off.

Hah! That's right! You can't leave me. I'm part of you

LARRY II: THE SQUEEQUEL

now. A permanent fixture like that foot on Sarah Jessica-Parker's face, or that horrible face on top of Mickey Rourke's old face. Try taking me off. Go on, have a go, see what happens.

Larry knew *exactly* what would happen; the mask *was* his face now. Who knew what mess lay beneath? He could peel the thing off only to discover a featureless ball. He had eyes. That much he was sure of, but Jocelyn Wildenstein had eyes; Rosie O'Donnell had eyes; Marilyn Manson had eyes – though one of them had cataracts, apparently. What Larry was trying to get at was: having eyes did not stop you from being utterly repulsive.

"Can we just stand here in silence, please?" Larry said, for he had a terrible migraine from all the walking and, no doubt, his mother's plaintive keening as he left. A small – *infinitesimal* – part of him had felt a pang of guilt at leaving his Ma alone in the cabin. You never knew what maniacs were out here in the woods, roaming about the place, looking for some harmless old woman to defile. Wilbur, though not much of a guard-pig, had been given strict instructions; '*see anyone with a weapon who isn't me, bite its fucking legs off.*'

Listen, said the mask. *You hear that?*

Larry's ears pricked up. He could hear the wind brushing past the trees, could hear the chittering of nocturnal insects and, if he listened really carefully, he could hear his mother, still wailing, because, if nothing else, Edie Travers was a cunning old minx.

"All I can hear is the wind brushing past the trees; the chittering of—"

Yes, yes, yes, said the mask. *None of that matters. Can you hear that other noise?*

Larry *could* hear it now. It sounded like the low growl of an engine, an engine in a car which had seen better days.

Stop picking your snout and hold your thumb out! said the mask.

Larry did just that. "Which way's it coming from?" he said. "I can't hear it properly over the wind brushing through the trees and the chittering of nocturnal insects. Not to mention MA! WILL YOU SHUT THE FUCK UP!? TRYING TO LISTEN OUT FOR CARS HERE! Sheesh."

Just then, the trees and road to his left lit up. Larry quickly pulled up his coat's hood and zipped it up to his eyes.

What are you doing? asked the mask. Do you think they're going to stop if they can't see your

LARRY II: THE SQUEEQUEL

face?

"Do you think they're going to stop if they *do* see my face?" Larry said, and he had a bloody good point.

The sound of music – though not that of the Von Trapp menagerie – drifted along the road as two perfectly-round and incredibly bright headlights appeared, attached to which was the rest of the car.

Thumb out! Act normal!

The car was less than ten feet away when Larry stepped out in front of it. Well, the fucking thing wasn't slowing down. Larry wasn't sure that the driver, a scared-looking chap with wide eyes and a screaming mouth (though he might only look like that when a hooded stranger stepped out in front of his speeding car in the middle of the night), had seen him. This was a sure-fire way to get noticed, though not the most practical.

Larry bounced off the car's bonnet, smashed the windshield with his body before somersaulting through the air and over the top of the spinning, screeching car. In hindsight, waiting for another car would have been far less painful.

He hit the tarmac at around the same time the swerving car fell off the side of the road, flipped once or twice, and came to a halt against a tree without a rudimentary penis scratched into it.

You've dropped your suitcase, said the mask.

"No shit!" Larry said, clambering to his feet. "Did you see that? That fucker almost killed me!" He made his way unsteadily toward his suitcase, which was twenty feet along the road, its contents spilled.

That's why you're only supposed to stick your thumb out! The mask sounded annoyed. *Stepping in front of moving vehicles almost always ends the same way.*

"Look at this mess." Larry dropped to his knees – which may or may not have been broken, it was too early to tell – and began stuffing his belongings back in the case. It was while he was rearranging his luggage that a small, bloody, and angry-looking man staggered up the embankment.

"Oi! *Prick*!"

Larry turned just as the injured man made it onto the road.

"What the fuck was *that*?" said the man. He was, Larry saw, limping as if he'd shit himself and holding onto his arm, as if afraid it might fall off if he didn't. "I mean, who steps in front of a moving car in the middle of the night? We're going to have to exchange insurance details. What's that?

LARRY II: THE SQUEEQUEL

Is that a fucking *axe*?"

He's sharp, innee? said the mask.

"Hang on a minute," the injured man said. "You're not…you're not Larry *Travers*, are you?"

Larry stood, axe clenched tightly in his hand, and removed his hood. The injured man's expression faltered, as one might expect it to when faced with certain death. He took a few steps back, whining something under his breath. He was, for want of a better word, *fucked*, and he knew it.

Larry rushed the man, axe already swinging in a wide arc. "*Squeeeeeeeeeee!*"

As the man's head bounced off one tree, and then another, before landing in a pile of guano, Larry was overwhelmed with emotions. It felt so good to be killing again. Oddly, he didn't get an erection, but it would have been even odder if he *had*, since his penis had been decimated in the conflagration up at Diamond Creek the previous year. There wasn't much left of it, at all. It looked like something you could buy in hundred-gram bags at a pet-store.

The injured man's body just stood there for a few seconds, as if confused. *Where's my head gone? I had it a moment ago.* Then it toppled forward, blood spurting from the stump of its neck, spraying the road.

Great, moaned the mask. *Drag that fucking mess off the road, before someone else comes along. And for God's sake put your penis away.*

"Does it look like a dog treat to you?"

It's disgusting. Just pull up your pants and get rid of that. Oh, I'm sorry, I was pointing. I forget…just get rid of it.

Larry pulled up his pants and dragged the headless body off the road. Kicking it down the embankment, he regarded the crumpled wreck with optimism.

Don't even think about it, said the mask. *You wouldn't know where to start. And besides, it's fucked. We'll just have to wait – probably forever – until another—*

"You looking for a ride, little piggy?" said a voice.

Larry snapped his head across and almost fell down the hill when he saw, sitting there, a dark blue pick-up. So silent and new was this jeep that neither he nor the mask had heard its approach. A woman hung out of the window. Her curly blonde hair and cowboy hat meant she was either a) a fan of country music b) on her way to some fancy-dress party, or c) Crocodile Dundee in drag.

Larry's inner monologue squeeeed, as was its

LARRY II: THE SQUEEQUEL

wont.

Don't kill this one, the mask reminded him. *At least until we get to Haddon.*

*

It transpired that the woman, whose name was Belle Boudoir — though that might have been a moniker, and not what was actually printed on her birth-certificate — was indeed on her way to a fancy-dress party. It also transpired that she had mistakenly assumed Larry was going to the same party. Why *else* would he be wearing a mask? Only people that went to fancy-dress parties wore masks. And gimps.

"D'you like Tammy Wynette, little piggy?" Belle asked, fiddling with the car's CD player.

"Never met her," Larry replied. "She *local*?"

"You're funny," Belle hooted as country music began to fill the pick-up. "Sure do like me a funny guy. D'ya think I'm *pretty*, little piggy."

Watch her, Larry. She's off her fucking tits.

Larry nodded. "*I* would," he said. *If I had anything remotely like a penis left to do it with*, he thought.

"You know, that's the sweetest thing a man has ever *said* to me," said the raging nymph. Larry didn't believe her, not for one minute. "So, how do you know Gerry and Jan?"

"Who?" Larry said.

The couple hosting this dress-up party, the mask reminded him. *Gerry and Jan Mayflower. Gerry's a doctor; Jan's a teacher, though she wants to go into criminal psychology one day. Fuck, Larry, haven't you been listening to a word this crazy broad's been saying?*

"I switched off," replied Larry.

"Excuse me?" Belle said.

"I said I had a *cough*," Larry said. "Gerry's my doctor."

"He's *great*, ain't he," said Belle. "He was the first guy I ever let put more than one finger in me." She burst out laughing, as if this was the funniest thing she'd ever said. Larry had no idea what she was talking about. "So, little piggy—"

"*Pigface*," Larry said, somewhat abruptly. "I prefer Pigface."

"Hm, *Pigface*," Belle said. "That sounds familiar." And for a few seconds, she simply stared at the road while she tried to recall where she had heard that name before.

If she twigs, said the mask, *you have my permission to put an axe in her head.*

"That's awfully kind of you," Larry said.

"Excuse me?" said Belle.

LARRY II: THE SQUEEQUEL

"I said I do a lot of charity work. That might be why you've heard of me."

"Maybe," she said. What passed, an uncomfortable silence, would have been far more uncomfortable if the women on the stereo hadn't been warbling on about how it wasn't God that made honky tonk angels, whatever the fuck *that* meant. Larry watched the trees rush by outside his window; even though they were miles away from where the woman had picked him up, Larry was almost certain he could still hear his mother wailing.

"Looks like it's going to rain," Belle said.

Larry was about to tell her he didn't give a shit about the weather when his entire body went into spasm and his head buzzed so hard, it put his Ma's moonshine to shame. And then…

*

There he was. That prick who had been up at the camp the previous year. The final girl's boyfriend, perhaps? In his hand was a shotgun. He obviously didn't know much about guns, for he was staring down the barrel of this one, turning it over and over as if looking for the on switch.

"You're going to shoot your own face off," said a voice, and Larry recognised it immediately.

The final girl.

"Don't be silly," said the boy. A moment later there was a flash and an almighty bang. When the debris settled, the boy said, "You'd better hold this. I'm going to shoot my own face off."

And then…

*

"…finished the night with a rim-job and a packet of Skittles."

"Huh?" Larry shook his head rapidly from side to side in an attempt to disperse the confusion. It didn't work.

Welcome back, numbnuts, said the mask.

"Then there was Barry Cletus," said Belle, without taking her eyes off the road. "Barry the Length, I liked to call him, on account that—"

"He had a massive cock?" Larry ventured.

"He liked to swim," said Belle. "So anyway, Barry booked us into this hotel for the weekend, you know? *Fancy* place it was, too, with the free biscuits and those dwarf shampoos. So anyway…"

And on and on she went, but Larry was no longer listening. He was running through his plan, which had consisted of killing the final girl, and maybe a couple of nonentities along the way – the Statute of Sequels Act 1981 demands that the body-count is higher, the kills more grisly, and the amount of breasticles on show doubled, or preferably tripled.

But now he had the boy to consider, too.

A smile curled up the corner of his lips.

And Belle concluded her story, another in a long line, with: "…and then we finished off with a blow-job and a cheese-and-tomato sandwich."

11
Elm Street

Amanda finished duct-taping the ceiling back into place (she liked the attic, but not enough to leave the thing open-plan) and climbed down from the ladder. Freddy, feeling somewhat sorry for himself, had settled in the corner of the room, browsing Amanda's small library with an expression of incredulity upon his countenance.

"Why do all of your books have topless men on them?" he said.

"They're *romance*," Amanda said, dusting off her bed. "All good romance books have topless men on the cover; it's how you know they're good."

They're *filth*, Freddy thought, sliding a particularly filthy one – kilt, sledgehammer, gasoline – back into its rightful place on the shelf.

"You're not *jealous*, are you?" Amanda said. "I mean, you and I...we had some *fun*, but that's all it was, you know?"

Freddy knew. Oh, he *knew* just fine. It's amazing how quickly a girl will throw herself at you in the woods when there's a raging psychopath in a pig-mask hacking people to death, but get her back to the city, where the chances of being hacked to death by *anyone*, let alone a psychopath in a pig-mask, are severely reduced, and you're immediately bumped down to the Friendzone, where you'd better reacquaint yourself with palm and her five sisters if you don't want to end up with a backlog…

"I know that," Freddy said. "We were scared, we needed comfort, one of us might have soiled ourselves, blah, blah, blah."

"Exactly," Amanda said. "So, we cool?"

Freddy nodded; inside, a little piece of him had died. "Yup," he lied.

"So where did you say you got the gun again?"

Freddy eased himself back in the chair – and it was one of those annoying teenager chairs, piled high with an array of cuddly toys that said teen had amassed over the years. It was a wonder Freddy wasn't on his ass on the floor. "I know a guy," he said, trying to sound mysterious but coming across as a bit of a cunt. "He's my uncle."

"And Uncle Peckinpah just handed it over?" Amanda said, examining the gun.

"He won't notice it's missing, if that's what you're getting at."

"Holy shit, Freddy! You took your uncle's gun

without telling him? That's…that's…"

"That's the only way we were going to get a gun," Freddy finished for her. "You said we needed weapons. I'm not Rutger Hauer, but I'm pretty sure that thing in your hand would blow a donkey's dick off from fifty yards."

"And miss everything you aim at from a hundred yards," Amanda said. "We're going to have to get up close and personal with Pigface to do him any real damage with this thing. Have you ever shot before?"

Freddy pointed up at the duct-taped ceiling. "You watched me do it," he said.

"Besides adding an extension to my bedroom?"

Freddy shook his head. "No, have you?"

"What do I look like, Grace Jones? Of course I haven't fired a gun before. I sit around in my bedroom all day reading softcore por…romance novels."

"So neither of us has experience with guns," Freddy said. "It doesn't matter. We don't even know if we *can* kill him to death with that thing. What if he's one of those relentless bastards? We already hacked him up and burnt him; even that wasn't enough. We might be barking up the wrong tree with weapons."

Amanda placed the shotgun gently on the bed and walked across the room. "What are you saying? That he might be immortal?"

Freddy sighed. "There's immortal, and then there's just persistent. If Pigface is going to keep coming back, no matter how many times we kill him, no matter how many bullets we put in him or how many limbs we chop off, then we need to think of something else. Think outside the box. Find a way to kill him once and for all, so that there's no chance of the franchise becoming stagnant."

"*Hate* when that happens," said Amanda.

"Yeah, like, know when to *stop*, assholes," Freddy snorted. "You can't just reboot the whole thing by putting your antagonist in outer space."

"Yeah."

"Ha, yeah."

"We sound like Beavis and Butthead now," Amanda said. "Let's get back on track."

"M'kay."

"So how do we kill him for good?" Amanda began rearranging her bookcase, for Freddy had made right pig's ear of it.

"Well, if Pigface is already dead, and after what

happened to him up at Diamond Creek, it's safe to assume he is, then we need to rid his reanimated body of the soul. Without the soul, the body can't function. We send his soul to Hell—"

"If there is such a place," Amanda said, for she liked nothing more than provoking the pious.

"—there's no way he can come back."

"So we need a *priest*?" Amanda turned to face Freddy. "One that's not destined for Hell, himself?"

"Let's go with a nun," Freddy said. "You never hear bad things about nuns."

"And where are we going to find a nun in Haddon?"

"—" said Freddy.

Amanda sighed and was about to head off in search of her copy of The Yellow Pages when…

"OH MY GOD!" she cried. Freddy almost fell off the cuddly-toy infested chair. "He's in a car! I can see everything through his eyes!"

"What can you see?" Freddy said, trying to ignore the fact that only the whites of Amanda's eyes were visible and that she looked as scary as shit.

"I see a road," she said.

"That figures," Freddy said. "What else can

you see?"

"There's a woman! Oh, Freddy, he's in a car with a woman! She's blonde, and wearing a cowboy hat! And she seems…seems to be simulating a blow-job on thin air!"

"Are you sure you're in Pigface's head?" Freddy said. "Is there any chance you've taken a wrong turn and ended up in the mind of Rob Zombie?"

"It's *him*!" Amanda squawked. "I'm looking out through the mask! I can see the edge of the eyeholes! Why's he not *killing* her right about now?"

"Maybe he *knows* her," Freddy said. "Ooh, ooh, *I* know. He needs a ride, *right*? If he's coming to Haddon, he needs a ride, and I'm guessing, living up there in the woods with nothing but an axe for company, he never took time out of his day to apply for driving lessons."

"GET OUT OF THERE!" Amanda screamed. Freddy stood, walked across the room, and pressed himself up against a wardrobe. The white-eyed stare of his former-girlfriend-cum-fuckbuddy had finally gotten to him. She looked possessed, or blind, or both. "He's going to kill her!" she went on. "When he gets to Haddon, he's going to *kill* her. I can feel his hatred for her, and she's not doing herself any favours, either, jabbering on like that."

"Can't you *do* something?" Freddy said from the edge of the room. "You're in his mind, aren't you? Convince him to open the door and toss himself out."

Amanda clenched her teeth and went, "*Gnnnnnnnngggghhhhhhh*". After around thirty seconds, and with an almost purple face, she said, "It's no good. I'm just a spectator along for the ride. Oh, it's stopped now." Her eyeballs rolled down into their proper position and the colour returned to her cheeks. A strange smell permeated the bedroom. "You'll have to excuse me for a moment," she said, mooching toward the door like John Wayne in any John Wayne film ever made. "There's something I have to take care of."

When she returned a whole fifteen minutes later, she was wearing a towel around her waist and a discomfited expression upon her face.

"*Nuns!*" Freddy said, intersecting what would otherwise have been an embarrassing moment. "We were about to find us a nun."

Amanda nodded. "We need to be quick about it," she said. "He's on his way. Where can we find a nun in Haddon at this time of night?"

LARRY II: THE SQUEEQUEL

*

"Hello, Haddon Nunnery, Daughters of Divine Charity, Sister Clarice speaking, how might I be of assistance?"

Amanda couldn't believe their luck. First of all, that such a place existed in their city. And secondly, that they had a nun manning (nunning?) the telephone at this ridiculous time. It was a little after ten. Shouldn't nuns be asleep by now, exhausted after a hard day of praying and not speaking to one another and collecting money out in the city centre to spend on their own bad habits (*bid-um-tish!*)?

"Yes, I was wondering whether you hire out your nuns?" Amanda said.

"Hire them *out*?" Sister Clarice said, her voice so shrill that Amanda had to keep the phone twelve inches from her ear. "What do you mean, 'hire them out'?"

"I *mean*," said Amanda, "is there any chance you've got a nun to spare for a couple of hours, only we've got a bit of a situation, and we need divine help."

"My dear, I don't know if this is some sort of wind-up, but if—"

"It's not a wind-up," Amanda interrupted. "We genuinely need a nun, or something terrible is going to happen to the people of Haddon."

"If this is about that new tanning salon, I've already made it perfectly clear that there is nothing we, The Sisters of Divine Charity, can do about it."

"It's not about the new tanning salon," Amanda said. "It's a matter of national emergency."

Freddy gave her a thumbs up. Those two words, national emergency, were usually enough to put the willies up anyone. Hopefully this nun had the willies up her.

"Listen, whateveryournameis—"

"Amanda," said she.

"Listen, Amanda. I'd be happy to loan you one of our nuns, if this is indeed a national emergency and you're not just going to make her strip or do anything silly."

"Oh, thank y—"

"On one condition," the nun said. "You talk her out of coming back here, to the convent. The other sisters and I have had enough of her. She is one of the worst nuns I've ever had the displeasure of meeting, and I'd be chuffed if you could convince her that she would be far better suited as, say, a mechanic, or a prisoner."

"We can do that," Amanda said. Freddy, unable

to hear the other end of the conversation, frowned and held his arms out: *do what?*

"In that case," said Sister Clarice, "you've got yourself a nun. I'll have her delivered to you first thing in the morning. And since you'll be doing us a favour, I'll throw in a couple of copies of the book for you."

"Oh, we already have copies of The Bible," Amanda said.

"Who said anything about The Bible?" Sister Clarice replied. "No, we've got a broom-cupboard full of *Fifty Shades of Grey*. People generously donate books for the cause, and that one seems to be pretty darn popular, though I've heard it's full of filth and sex and terrible writing. Since the sisters and I are celibate, and I'd hate for my girls to become aroused after all these years abstinence, I've been stockpiling them and trying to get rid of them."

"Have you considered a bonfire?" Amanda said.

"I *did*," Sister Clarice said, "but the books, for some reason, are extremely damp. It would be like trying to set fire to a walrus."

"Well, it's been lovely talking to you," Amanda said, trying to draw a line under the conversation.

"We look forward to receiving our mail-order nun in the morning. My address is—"

"1203 Elm Street," Sister Clarice said. "There, that saved a sentence or two, didn't it? Oh, and Sister Geoff can be a bit of a handful, and she has to have her methadone before ten, otherwise she goes batshit cray-zee. Goodbye." *Beeeeeeeeeeeeeeeeeeep.*

Amanda slowly lowered the phone back into its cradle.

"Did I hear the word 'methadone' at the end there?" Freddy said.

"You did," said Amanda. "But I'm sure it was just a joke. I mean, nuns have a sense of humour, right?"

"Not *really*," Freddy said. "So do we have a nun, or do we have a nun?"

"We have…*something*," Amanda said. A drug-addled mechanic in nun's clothing, by the sounds of it. "In the meantime, I think we should go to bed."

Freddy's eyes lit up, but only for a second or two. "You're right," he said. "But we should keep watch. If Pigface is already on his way to Haddon, he'll be here before midnight."

"Good thinking," said Amanda, yawning. "You

take first watch. Let's just hope our nun arrives before Pigface does." Though, from what she'd gleaned during the telephone call to Haddon Nunnery, both were as bad as one another.

12
The Mayflower Residence (just before Midnight)

Belle Boudoir slowed the car, located a space along the kerb and, after ten minutes of trying, managed to reverse-park into it. Larry glared out of the passenger window at the huge house at the end of the huge drive. You could, he thought, fit a hundred cabins in there and still have space for a dozen pigsties.

"Are we in Haddon?" he said. "Is this…is *this* Haddon?"

Belle regarded him the way she might a retarded little brother. "We're on the outskirts," she said. "Haddon's a few miles that way." All of a sudden she looked confused. "I thought you said Gerry was your doctor?"

Say something, urged the mask.

"Whatever happened to Amelia Earhart?" said Larry.

About Gerry, chided the mask.

"Oh, erm, Gerry *is* my doctor, but I've never been to his house before." Larry just wanted to put an axe in this bitch's head and be done with it, but he could sense the mask's apprehension. They

LARRY II: THE SQUEEQUEL

might need this woman for transport purposes later, for Larry didn't have the foggiest where they were, or how far it really was to Haddon. 'A few miles' Belle had said, which could be anything between two and fifty out here in the sticks.

"What did happen to Amelia Earhart?" Belle said, turning the engine off and opening her door. "Bitch just vanished into thin air." She climbed out of the car. The mask saw this as a good time for a quick word, though why it had waited until now was beyond Larry. It wasn't as if anyone else could hear it.

Okay, so this is a party where everyone is dressed up, m'kay? Luckily, we'll fit right in. We're in their world now, and it's a little different to ours. They have real beer, not stuff strained through an old sock, and they like loud music – the louder the better – and dance funny to it, I think it's called Turding, or something...

"I'm going to have to kill them all," Larry muttered.

No! said the mask. *Absolutely not. If you want to hunt down and slash that bitch and her boyfriend to death, you're going to have to keep a low profile. Butchering a houseful of guests at a party is not the best way to go about it.*

Groaning, and swearing, Larry eased himself

out of the car and slammed the door shut. Belle was already staggering up the path toward the house. It was only now that he noticed her legs. Not that she had a pair – how *else* would she be able to drive the car? – but that they went most of the way up her body. "Come on, little piggy," she called across her shoulder. "Let's go and have some fun!"

Ma was right, Larry thought. City life was not for him.

*

"There's somebody at the door!" sang everyone inside the house as the doorbell chimed. It had become their little thing – bunch of annoying and pretentious fucks, they were – and signalled the arrival of yet another guest to the Mayflower party.

"I'll get it," said the man in the TMNT costume. Gerry Mayflower whirled from the drink's table and stalked across the room, a hero in a half-shell, toward the door. On the way he passed a Transformer, Pikachu, a pair of Power Rangers, the Dalai Lama, Patrick Swayze – who wasn't there a second later, and might have just popped in for a giggle – The Mad Hatter, a trio of Batmen, one Spiderman (who wasn't even invited), and a naked pirate (who wouldn't be invited to the next one).

LARRY II: THE SQUEEQUEL

It was a good party, and would only get better as the night progressed. Once they started throwing their keys into the bowl on the coffee-table and…

"Welcome!" Gerry said, yanking the door open and doing something really fiddly with a pair of nunchuks. So fiddly was his manoeuvre that he almost blinded the cowgirl on the step before thwacking himself a right royal cropper in the gonads. It knocked him bandy but, as they say in the business – though not in the funeral business – 'the show must go on'. And on it went, albeit with a slightly pained expression and a husky moan. "Belle…how…how wonderful to see…you."

"You too, Gerry," she said, leaning in for a kiss and a cuddle. Gerry offered to take her hat, jacket, and tights, but since that was all she was wearing, she respectfully declined.

"And who's *this* little pork scratching?" said Gerry, turning his attention to Larry, who now donned his trademark white apron, replete with blood-spatter and brain-matter.

"This is Larry," said Belle. "You two already know each other. Larry is one of your patients."

And we're fucked already, said the mask. *I thought we'd at least get to have a proper drink, one that didn't give us the shits.*

"Larry?" said Gerry, stroking his chin but being careful not to wipe his green face-paint off. "Larry? Larry-Larry-Larry…"

"That's me," said Larry.

"Not… *VD* Larry?"

Tell him yes, said the mask.

"Yup, that's me," he said.

"Really?" said Belle, seemingly upset. "You could have told me that before you got in the car."

"Wow, I haven't heard from you for *months*," said Gerry. "I take it the old pecker's on the mend?"

Larry nodded. "Never better," he said, if better meant 'a scabrous little black thing that gave off a strange smell and looked apt to drop off at any moment'.

"Come in, come in!" Gerry said, as if suddenly remembering his manners. "Jan!" he called into the living room. "Belle's here, and she's brought VD Larry!"

Everyone turned to stare at the newcomers; the music stopped, as it often did when you didn't want it to, and a woman dressed in bondage gear stood up from the sofa and removed the ball-gag from her mouth. "So good to see you both," said the woman. "Take it the old pecker's on the mend, Larry?"

"Never better," said Larry, if better meant, well, you get the idea.

"Here you go," Gerry said, handing Larry a glass of something pink and clear – the exact opposite of what he was used to at home. "Get that down your neck."

Just then, Jan appeared and stole Belle away into the crowd, leaving Larry and Gerry alone.

"Great party, *huh*?" Gerry said, motioning to the madness taking place all around. "Jan wanted to make it *Star Trek* themed; can you believe that? I mean, who wants to fuck a Klingon?"

"I have absolutely no idea what you're talking about," Larry said, knocking back his pink cocktail. "So I'm just going to nod from here on in." As if to demonstrate, he began to nod.

"So, how do you know Belle?" Gerry said, swinging one of his nunchuks around his head. It was, Larry thought, quite disconcerting.

"I don't," he said.

You do! said the mask. *Tell him you do!*

"I do," he quickly corrected.

"*How*, though?" asked Gerry.

Tell him something believable, the mask urged.

"She's my cousin," said Larry. "Well, second-cousin, twice-removed, and all that…technically, we're not even related. Just ships passing in the night."

Stop talking, said the mask, and so Larry shut the fuck up.

"You know," said Gerry, "I've almost forgotten what you look like." He craned his neck, as if trying to catch a glimpse through the mask's eyeholes. "Take the mask off for a moment, yeah? I feel weird chatting to such an ugly mask."

Changed my mind, said the mask. *You can hack up the fucking lot of 'em.*

Larry stood in silence, unsure of what to say. He couldn't take the mask off. It was as much a part of him as his blackened winkle.

"Larry?" said Gerry. "Take off the mask."

"I can't," Larry said.

"You *can*."

"I can't."

"Larry, take off the mask now. What's the big fucking *deal*?" And with that, Gerry reached up and grasped onto a porcine ear. "Take it—"

What happened next was so *horrible* that it deserves a warning. Those with a dicky tummy or a nervous disposition should skip the remainder

LARRY II: THE SQUEEQUEL

of this chapter.

Larry, feeling the tug on his ear, knew he had to do something; that he had been backed into a corner from which there was no way out. He pulled back his arm, aware that he was still grasping a glass that had previously contained a pink cocktail so sweet it had set all six of his false teeth on edge. He thrust his hand forward as hard as he could, smashing the glass into Gerry's giant, green face. Blood geysered out almost immediately, and for a moment, Larry stood enjoying it.

Then people started screaming and losing their shit, which was about the reaction Larry expected.

You've done it now, scolded the mask.

"Good job I brought this," Larry said. He reached around to his back and pulled the axe from the waistband of his trousers. "*Squeeeeeeeeeee!*"

A Power Ranger – though Larry didn't know that; to him it was just some dude in blue lycra – lunged toward Larry, spilling his beer in the process. Larry brought the axe around in a wide arc, and the blue Power Ranger (everyone's least favourite anyway, so, hey ho!) tottered forward, trying to figure out where his right arm had gone. Another swing of the axe decapitated the poor bastard, his fibreglass helmet smashing as it impacted the far wall.

More screams filled the house as costumed people began to rush toward the door, but Larry wasn't about to let any of them leave.

Oooh, get the Smurf! said the mask, seemingly over its no-kill policy.

Larry rushed out to the hallway, where bodies were pressed up against the door, trying to figure out how to work the chain. "*Squeeeeeeee!*" said he, which was as much a catchphrase now as, "Pow! Right in the kisser," and, "Is that your final answer?" He began hacking away at the backs of those trying to escape. "*Gnfh*," said one man. "*Heeeeeeelp!*" said another. "Surely *one* of you knows how to work this bloody chain!" said a third.

Someone – a Disney Princess, judging by the way she was dressed – leapt onto Larry's back, wrapped her legs around his waist, and began slapping at his head with both hands. "Fucking with the wrong Cinderella!" she said, and had taken to chewing on his right ear.

White spots danced across Larry's vision, but he refused to be bettered by someone who deemed glass slippers a perfectly acceptable form of footwear. He staggered backwards, pressing

LARRY II: THE SQUEEQUEL

Cinderella against the wall and knocking the wind out of her. "Squeeeeeeeeeeeee!" he wailed, turned the axe around so that the blade faced him. He swung upwards, and there was a meaty *thunk!* as it embedded in Cinders' head. After that, the fight pretty much went out of her.

Yanking the axe from the princess's head, and watching as she crumpled to the floor, Larry turned to the sea of bloody bodies still trying to figure out how to escape.

There are too many of them! said the mask. *Improvise!*

Larry rushed into the living room, where he was met with a drink's tray to the face. On the end of the tray, Jan Mayflower looked rather annoyed that her party had descended into chaos, and a little upset that her husband of eighteen years now sported a cocktail glass where his right eye used to be.

"You killed my *husband!*" she screamed, wielding the tray as if it were a shield and she was one of three-hundred Spartans. The ball-gag swinging around her face did detract a little from the illusion, but Larry was too busy seeing stars to notice it. "After all he did for you and your VD."

She was about to crack Larry another good one

when he came to. "Squeeeeeee!" he said, and brought the axe down on Jan Mayflower, splitting her in two down to her shoulders. As one side of her head went one way, and the other side went the other, Larry pulled out the axe and continued to the kitchen, where a giant rabbit, an elderly gentleman dressed as the Pope, and a Michael Jackson were all hammering at the back door. One man, a fat fucker who hadn't bothered with the formality of dressing up (unless he'd come as a fat fuck) was sat at the buffet table. When he saw Larry in the kitchen doorway, he pushed two sausage-rolls into his fat face and began to chew frantically. Oh, if he was going to die, he was going to die full…

"Squeeeeeee!" Larry said, and launched his axe toward the back door, where it thumped into Michael Jackson's back.

"OW! Heeee-heeee," said Jacko, before falling to one side.

Larry wasted no time in retrieving his axe. At the front of the house, something smashed.

They're escaping through the windows! the mask said. *Can't let them get away, Larry. They'll fuck up our whole agenda.*

Larry knew the mask was right, and so he had

LARRY II: THE SQUEEQUEL

to work quickly. After a bit of a wrestle with the giant rabbit – which left the rabbit with a broken back, two broken arms, and a severed tail – Larry dragged the cooker out and raised his axe. He slammed it down, severing the pipe connecting the cooker to the main gas-line. After a few seconds, the sickly stench of gas had filled the kitchen.

Oh, Larry, I didn't mean blow the place—

Larry pushed the ignitor on the cooker, and there was a tiny *click-click-click*, followed by a spark, followed by…

*

Three miles away, Derrick and Davina Jett were making love in their king-size bed. They had been married for seventy-two years, and so nights like this didn't come around as often as they used to. After much fumbling and the removal of boiled sweets, Derrick had managed to penetrate Davina, his perpetually-flaccid penis pushing through the wall of cobwebs as if it were Indiana Jones on a search for the Lost Ark of the Covenant. After assuring his wife that, yes, it was in, and yes, he had remembered to put the trash out, Derrick Jett went at her like a jackhammer, albeit one on the blink. It was while Davina Jett considered which numbers to play on the Lottery next week, and while Derrick Jett thought back to the previous Sunday, when he'd caught a 60lb brown trout down at the lake, that the room began to shake. Pictures fell from walls; dust fell from the ceiling; their cat, Jezebel, fell from her rightful place on the mantelpiece and landed in the fire, but it was okay, for she had been stuffed for twenty years and didn't feel a thing.

When everything fell still once again, Derrick Jett removed his penis, tapped it once or twice on Davina's inner thigh, and said, "You're very welcome."

*

Three miles in the other direction, Sam Treat and Martha Blankenship had just checked into their hotel after a night of wild partying. Sam, however, had decided upon an early night, for tomorrow was the Harry Hunter party and she wanted to be up bright and early in order to get her arse waxed.

"Martha," said Sam, climbing into bed and pulling a mask down over her eyes.

"Sam?" said Martha, oiling up her body with cream until she looked like something you put in the oven at gas mark 7.

"Set an alarm for nine, would you? Busy day tomorrow."

LARRY II: THE SQUEEQUEL

Martha nodded, gave Sam the middle finger – which was risky, but she didn't think the bitch could see through her eye-mask – and reached for her mobile-phone-cum-alarm-clock.

Just then, there was a loud bang, and Martha's heart leapt up into her throat.

"And Martha?" said Sam.

"Yes?" Martha said, shaking a little.

"If you're going to be flatulent all night long, can you go and book yourself into another room?"

*

Eric Roberts sat up his tree, sharpening his throwing-stars and pondering upon how *Sleeping with the Enemy* was such a critical success. "It's 'cos she got fucked in it," he mumbled. "Yeah, that's what it was. Good ol' Julia, always willing to go that extra mile for directors. Fucking bitch." He ran his finger along the newly-sharpened edge of the star and, when he saw the blood emerge from a slit in his finger, he knew the job was a good un.

He was about to settle down for the night when a loud bang sent him tumbling from the tree. "Ow!" he said, climbing to his feet and pulling the shuriken from his ass. "Can't a guy take a day off around here?"

After searching the perimeter of the alleyway,

and finding nothing but a dead 'coon and a candy wrapper which hadn't been there an hour ago, he climbed back up his tree, where he dreamt that Hollywood hadn't lost his number, after all.

*

Sister Clarice had just tidied up the *Fifty Shades of Grey* cupboard when the distant explosion rattled the foundations of Haddon Nunnery. "No, no, no, no!" gasped the nun, but it was too late. A sea of books surged from the cupboard, their insipid covers causing bile to rise in the nun's throat.

"Fucksticks!" said the nun, for as religious as she was, she knew when God was having a laugh at her expense.

*

Mayor Johnnie Ketchum was as pissed as a newt and, like the rest of the patrons of Lou's Bar, did nothing to hide the fact. Shirts were untucked, vomit flowed freely, penises were exposed, and money spent as if it was going out of fashion. Tomorrow morning he would wake with the unholiest of headaches, but that was fine as he only had a Burger King, a RadioShack, and three new barbershops to unveil. If he couldn't do that while half-cut, then his name wasn't Mayor Johnnie Ketchum.

LARRY II: THE SQUEEQUEL

"Hey, Mayor," Lou said, wiping a dirty glass with an even dirtier dishcloth. "You got any of those 2for1 tanning vouchers left. It's my wife's birthday next week and I don't know what to get her."

Johnnie reached into his back pocket, which wasn't terribly difficult as he'd already removed his trousers and set them on the bar in front of him. "Hergh…how merny?" said he, in that internationally-recognised language known as *Pissedish*.

"She's a big lady, you know? Lot of field to crop-dust, if you catch my drift," Lou said. "Better make it a dozen."

Johnnie began to count out a dozen vouchers, even though he'd forgotten how many a dozen was. In the end, he handed Lou thirty-seven of the little fliers. "Tell…guh…tell Mrs Lou…herpy berfday."

"Will do, Mayor," Lou said, putting the vouchers in the register.

Suddenly, the entire bar trembled. Glasses chittered along the bar as if they had become independent of their drinkers. A bowl of peanuts, already precariously balanced on the end of one of the tables, finally gave up the ghost and committed nuticide.

"Wahey!" cheered the mayor. "Earfquerk!" Then he slammed back a straight whiskey, ordered three more of the same, before passing out in the toilet mid-piss.

*

Freddy's eyes snapped open, and for a moment he didn't have a clue where he was. Then he felt the Cuddle-me-Elmo behind him, and it all come flooding back. Had he fallen asleep? He must have, though he couldn't remember it. In that case, what had woke up him? A loud bang, of some sort? Had he farted himself awake? That was *always* embarrassing.

He turned toward the bed and was pleased to see, through the gloom, that Amanda slept on. God, she looked beautiful. Pity she was snoring like a sailor with emphysema. Still, part of him wanted to climb into bed with her. Just for a cuddle. The night had grown cold, and the Bateman house was old and big and *sans* radiators.

She looks so warm, thought Freddy. *So warm, like a taxidermy cat on a roaring log-fire*, though where that simile came from he had no idea.

He pushed himself slowly up from the chair, sending plush bears and crocheted hand-puppets

LARRY II: THE SQUEEQUEL

overboard.

If I could just get into the bottom of the bed, he thought, eyeing it up and licking his lips. *She won't mind if she wakes up and we're top-to-toe. She'll probably thank me, tell me it was nice, that my body-heat had—*

"Don't even *think* about it," a voice grunted from the darkness.

Freddy returned to his chair in a huff and shivering like a shitting Chihuahua.

*

Larry, now lying in the Mayflower back garden, removed a smouldering door from his legs and climbed to his feet. The heat from the burning house in front of him was almost unbearable.

A naked pirate ran past, squealing and more than a little bit on fire. He made it halfway across the blackened lawn before falling forwards onto his face, where he twitched once or twice before falling very still.

In the distance, sirens wailed in the night (not to be confused with Captain Ahab, who also whaled in the night).

Better skedaddle, said the mask.

And skedaddle Larry did.

13
1203 Elm Street – The Morning After Larry Made a Crater

There came a knock at the door. It was the kind of knock designed to wake sleeping people, and thusly both Amanda and Freddy jumped up and ran about the place, confused and still full of sleep.

"What time is it?" Amanda said, unable to focus on her watch's small face.

"Seven," Freddy said. He had a man's watch – the kind of watch you could hang on the wall and call a clock.

"*Seven*? Who the bloody hell could be calling at this time of a morning?"

Freddy shrugged, picked up the shotgun, and peeked out onto the landing. "What if it's Pigface?" he said. "It's too early for a fight." And he was right; we've all been there. Scrapping is usually the last thing one wants in those moments following slumber. Your limbs are all floppy, and you're still struggling to keep your eyes open. Plus, you haven't been to the toilet yet…

Amanda shook her head. "I think I would have felt it," she said, loathing the fact she was somehow twinned with a merciless butcher. "The nun!" she added, suddenly recalling the previous night's telephone conversation.

"Bit early for a nun, isn't it?" Freddy lowered the shotgun. "I thought they had to shit, shower, shave, and pray first."

Amanda pushed past Freddy and headed down the stairs. Freddy followed, though he wasn't giving up the shotgun just yet. If it was a nun, well, she just had to come to terms with being a nun with a shotgun pointing at her.

"Hello?" Amanda said through the door. "Who is it, please?"

There was a slight pause, and then a gruff, somewhat masculine, voice said, "Who the fuck d'ya think it is, you daft trout? Some saft fucker ordered a nun, now if you don't mind letting me in and telling me what all this nonsense is about, I've got to get to the chemist for nine, and then a party this afternoon up at the Hunter mansion, so tick-tock, and all that bollocks."

Amanda unbolted the door, turned the key, slipped the chain across – unlike the Mayflower guests, who had seen it as some kind of unsolvable puzzle – and eased the door open. As soon as there was a gap wide enough, the nun waddled through it, barging Amanda aside. Once in the hallway, the nun turned on Freddy and said, "That a shotgun, boy? D'ya mind not pointing it at me, unless you like hospital food?"

Freddy lowered the weapon, and also his bowels.

Amanda closed the door and made it secure once again.

"So," said the nun. "What the actual fuck do you pair of cunts want with me? Huh?"

"You must be Sister Geoff," Amanda said.

"And *what?*" said Sister Geoff. "Who you been talking to? Whatever they said I did, I didn't." The stench of stale alcohol filled the hallway, and it was only then that Amanda saw the cigarette tucked behind the nun's cauliflower ear.

"We need your help," Freddy said, slotting the shotgun into an antique umbrella rack.

"I don't do abortions," said the nun, motioning to Amanda's belly. "Stopped doing 'em years ago, after it all kicked off in the Vatican. No, if you're looking to get rid of a baby, you're gonna have to wait until it's born and take it down the skip like everyone else."

"We're not looking for an abortion," Amanda said.

"Why would you wanna keep a baby in this day

and age?" Sister Geoff said, reaching up for the cigarette and stuffing it into her puckered lips. "What with all the paedos knocking about the place. I remember a time you could let your kid get in a car with a complete stranger and they wouldn't get buggered. When I was a little nun—"

"Look, we're quite pressed for time," Amanda said. There was something about Sister Geoff which frightened her, and it wasn't just the cauliflower ears and broken nose, and she hated to interrupt, but they were, in fact, pressed for time. "We need you to help us locate a pig-faced slasher and then banish his soul from the body, which is nothing more than a vessel, now, since we watched him die last year. Only he's come back, voodoo probably, and we don't know what else to try."

Sister Geoff took it all in, only stopping to light her cigarette. After thirty seconds of head-scratching, the nun said, "It'll cost ya."

"Well, how much are we looking at?" Freddy said, aware that neither he nor Amanda were incredibly well-off. "We're not incredibly well-off."

"Either of you have any weed contacts?" said the nun, regarding them both in turn. "You look like you've smoked a bit in your time," she told Freddy. "Hook me up with a regular dealer –

mine's just gone down for tax evasion, and by tax evasion I mean first-degree murder. You hook me up with a dealer, I'll help you exorcise this pig-faced killer and send him on his merry way to Hell."

"Deal," Amanda said.

"You're on," Freddy added, trying to remember the name of the kid he once bought a joint from in woodwork class.

Sister Geoff reached across and pulled the shotgun out of the umbrella rack. "I don't think this will be any use at all," she said, stuffing it into her tunic.

"Then why are we taking it?" Amanda said.

"Well, I don't know whether tiddler-breath's" — she pointed at Freddy — "dealer is going to try to sell me coriander, now, *do* I?"

Amanda was about to reply when her eyes rolled back in her face and she made a low thrumming sound in her throat.

"Fuck me," said Sister Geoff. "What's the matter with her?"

Freddy, taking a few steps back, said, "It's been happening on and off since she mentally bonded with our killer. It'll pass in a minute."

"I bloody hope so," said the nun. "She's giving

me the shits, and nothing frightens me. I went to a Catholic school."

"So what made you want to become a nun?" Freddy asked, looking anywhere but the creepy face of his former girlfriend, who had now gone into spasm.

"I didn't have much choice," Sister Geoff said. "I was left on the convent doorstep, wrapped in a blanket."

"People still *do* that?"

"They did fifty years ago. Look, is she going to be alright? I mean, should we punch her in the face or something?"

"No, no, she'll come to in a minute," Freddy said. "So, are there any lesbians in your convent?"

"Most of 'em," Sister Geoff said. "I'm one of the only ones that likes a bit of cock."

"That's nice," said Freddy, though it really wasn't. "And do you—"

"What's with all the questions, cuntybollocks?" Sister Geoff said. "You working for the Feds or something?"

Freddy dry-swallowed. "I'm just *interested*," he said. "I've never had a chance to speak to a real-life nun before. I've seen plenty of your kind—"

"My kind? My *kind*? Son, do I look like a

Hispanic to you?"

"Tad racist," Freddy muttered.

"Didn't think so," said Sister Geoff, settling once again, and now checking her watch, which wasn't a man's watch, surprisingly. "If she doesn't knock it off in the next thirty seconds, I'm going to have to slap her. If I don't get my methadone on time, 9am sharp—"

"You go cray-zeee," Freddy finished for her. "Don't worry, she'll snap out of it any sec—"

"He's in a skip!" Amanda squealed.

"Told you so," Freddy said to Sister Geoff.

"Who's in a skip?" Sister Geoff said.

"Pigface," said Amanda.

"*What* skip?" said Sister Geoff. She was under the impression that she could waltz on out to the skip, perform an exorcism on it and its contents, fire a few rounds into it, just to be sure, put in her prescription, fuck off over to Harry Hunter's party where things were bound to get messier than a bunch of incontinent seniors on curry night, before heading back to the convent with a bag of weed large enough to daze an elephant. Not bad for a day's work, and part of the reason she became a nun in the first place.

"I don't know *what* skip," said Amanda.

LARRY II: THE SQUEEQUEL

"Fucksticks," Sister Geoff said. It was the Daughters of Divine Charity's favourite curse word. That and Womblecock.

"Were there any clues?" Freddy asked.

"Banana skins, used condoms, smashed bottles, lots of smelly stuff, nothing useful." Amanda rubbed the sleep from her eyes; it was too early in the morning for psychopath visions.

"If he's in a skip," Freddy said, "then he must already be in the city."

"We have to find him and destroy him," Amanda said.

"*Matrix*?" Freddy said.

"Yeah, great line."

"I need my methadone."

"Come on."

"Let's go."

"I have to take a piss."

"Take a piss then."

And so on and so forth. It was fifteen minutes later when they left the house. Two teens and a rogue nun, off in search of a pig-faced slasher. Seriously, you couldn't make this stuff up.

14
A Mystery Skip

Glad you could join us, said the mask as Larry opened his eyes. Head pounding, he eased himself up into a sitting position, then quickly repositioned himself as something sharp embedded itself in his backside. He pulled the used syringe out of his ass and tossed it aside. "Where are we? It *stinks*."

Oh, that's right, said the mask, sounding like an angry wife. *You were too pissed last night to even remember climbing into the skip. I didn't even get a 'goodnight' or a peck on the cheek. Sometimes, I don't think you love me anymore…*

"What the hell are you babbling on about?" Larry said, glad to find he was still in possession of his axe.

So you don't remember drinking that fizzy pink stuff and then ramming your glass into Gerry Mayflower's eye?

"I remember *that*," he said. "And I remember blowing up their house, but after that…" He trailed off, because after that he couldn't remember diddlysquat.

Well, allow me to fill you in, said the mask, its tone suggesting that if it had arms, they would have been firmly folded across its chest. *After you decided*

LARRY II: THE SQUEEQUEL

to blow yourself up, the police and fire-brigade arrived at the house — or the space in the road where there used to be a house. We were hiding in the bushes out back, and I told you to stay put until the 5-0 had done their thing, only you refused to wait. You wanted to tell the police how much you loved them, that you wanted to sit in the front seat of their car and play with the siren—

"What was in that pink drink?"

Oh, it gets better, said the mask. *So out you pop from the bushes, still smoking from the explosion, and over you go to the cops who are trying to figure out what had happened, and why there were bits of giant rabbit lying about the place.*

"Why didn't they shoot me?"

They did *shoot you. Multiple times. You've never had so much lead in you.*

"And I'm not dead?"

Does this look like Hell to you? I mean, this is pretty nasty, but Hitler would trade places with you right now, given half a chance. So anyway, after getting yourself shot to smithereens, you decided to take out eight police officers, four firemen, and a woman who just happened to be walking her dog at the time.

"Did I kill the dog?"

Of course you killed the dog! You're a slasher. What kind of slasher doesn't kill the dog?

"Good point."

Once everything with a heartbeat was dead or dying, you collected your suitcase from the nympho's car and got the hell out of there.

Larry relaxed a little, the way any good drunk does upon waking and discovering that nothing crazy happened the night before. "So where are we now?"

We, said the mask, *are in a skip on the edge of Haddon. You decided to have a little lie down, sleep off the pink stuff and let the bullet-holes heal.*

"I'm never drinking something that hasn't been strained through a dirty sock ever again," said Larry. "My head is fucking killing me."

You did, as the bishop said to the bishop's wife, take a shot to the face.

Larry spat out a bullet. It chinked against a tin can before disappearing amongst the rubble. "This is good," he said. "Not the bit about lying in a skip; the bit about not being dead."

Yeah. Luckily for you this is Part Two in what hopefully doesn't turn into a franchise. If this was Part One, you'd be pushing up daisies by now.

Larry arched his back. "On the outskirts of Haddon, you say?"

I did say that, replied the mask.

LARRY II: THE SQUEEQUEL

"Which means we're not far from that bitch and her boyfriend."

I didn't say that, but you're on the right track.

"So what do we do now, other than kill more people, thusly creating a much bigger body count, as is often the case in unnecessary sequels?"

Well, you could start by getting us the fuck out of this skip, said the mask.

"Righty-ho," said Larry, and out of the skip he got them.

15
Haddon General Pharmacy

"Ah, Sister Geoff," said the pharmacist – a small stocky man with wayward eyes, a large nose, and thin, almost non-existent, lips. In short, he had a face only a mother could love, and even then only in small doses. "The usual, is it?"

Sister Geoff sighed. "No, I thought I'd have a change today," said she. "Let's skip the methadone. I'll have a box of Ny-Ny, a litre of Robitussin, and a dozen condoms, preferably ribbed for my pleasure, and…" She trailed off as the pharmacist disappeared into the back, off in search of Sister Geoff's methadone. To Amanda and Freddy, the nun said, "Don't you think he's got a face only a mother could love?"

"Only in small doses," said Freddy. "Look is this going to take long?"

"It'll take a lot longer if you keep badgering me," Sister Geoff said. "And besides, do you know how many skips there are in Haddon? Needle in a haystack doesn't even come close to it. More like atom at a rock concert. Grain of sand in a library—"

"Piece of real cheese at a fake cheese

convention."

"Who said you could play?" Sister Geoff turned on Amanda. "Anyway, what I'm trying to say is that we've got to wait for your psychotic slasher to emerge before we go looking for him. I hate to say it, but we need to wait until Little Miss Scary-White-Eyes here has another vision."

Freddy shuddered.

"What happens when we get him?" Amanda said. "You are trained in the art of exorcism, aren't you?"

Sister Geoff snorted. "Trained...*trained* in the *art*...of exorcism." She was laughing now, in that unsettling way nuns do when they know something you don't. "Dear, you can't be *trained* in something that the Vatican no longer endorses."

"But you *are*, though, aren't you?"

"I've got a certificate, yes," said the nun. "Even got a Blue Peter badge, but that's neither here nor there. All you need to know is that, when the time comes, I'll make that sonofabitch wish he'd never been reborn."

"One double-dose of methadone for Sister Geoff," said the facially-retarded pharmacist as he emerged from the back area.

"*Double*-dose?" Amanda said. "You're not

going to be smacked off your tits, are you?"

Sister Geoff twisted the cap off the bottle and necked its contents in one. "I wish," she said, handing the empty bottle back to the pharmacist.

"How's that mistress of yours," asked the man behind the counter. "Clarice, isn't it?"

"Still celibate," Sister Geoff informed him.

"Pity. Well, be sure to let me know when it's a good time to take a run at her."

"Will do," said the nun, turning and making for the door. "Give my love to your mother, Frank."

"Would do," said Frank the Pharmacist. "She's not talking to me at the moment. Sometimes, I think she only loves me—"

"In small doses," Sister Geoff finished for him before marching out onto the street, her new friends in tow.

LARRY II: THE SQUEEQUEL

16
Lou's Bar

When Lou came downstairs that morning to clean up the mess from the night before, he'd expected to find bits of broken glass everywhere, spilled beer, torn clothes from the seven fights he'd witnessed, a smashed slot-machine, a pool-table with its felt half-off, a pair of broken pool cues, and several rats eating the suicidal nuts from the floor. He wasn't disappointed, in that sense, however he got quite the shock of his life when, upon entering the ablutions, a man wearing toilet-paper on his forehead and wielding a plunger leapt out from one of the cubicles, screaming at the top of his lungs about opening up a Burger King.

"Mayor Ketchum!" Lou said. "Put the plunger down! You're going to unblock somebody, if you're not careful."

The mayor glanced about the place, a look of utter confusion furrowing his brow. "Must…have…asleep…fallen," he said, which wasn't exactly right, but it was close enough.

"You've got a turd on your shoulder," said Lou, pointing toward the offending nugget. Johnnie shook it off before turning to face one of the broken mirrors lining the wall. "Fuck, Lou, look at the state of me. I've got *places* to open, ribbons to cut, people to disappoint."

Lou shook his head. "You've got bigger problems than opening up some rat-infested eatery today, Johnnie," he said.

The mayor peeled the toilet paper from his forehead and said, "Uh?"

"You haven't *heard?*"

"Lou, I've been lying in a cubicle covered in *shit* for the last eight hours. How could I have heard anything?"

"Get yourself cleaned up and meet me out in the bar," said Lou. "You always said nothing exciting never happened in Haddon. I'm pretty sure your wish just came true." And with that, he turned and left.

"Bit dramatic," said the mayor, sniffing his shirt-sleeve.

*

"Haddoners are waking up this morning, some in bar toilets, to the terrible news that a massacre has claimed the lives of at least thirty people in a house at the edge of Haddon. Police officers and the fire department were dispatched to the premises at a little after midnight following reports of a loud explosion nearby, and were never heard from again. A second group of officers arrived at the scene shortly after 2am to discover what one officer referred to as 'an absolute mess'. Another officer backed up his colleague's summation with the following statement."

Cut to a nervous-looking HPD boy-in-blue who, according to the graphic on screen, vomited several times at the scene, rendering any forensic evidence inadmissible in court.

"We arrived at the house at just after two this morning," he said, clearly struggling. "I've never seen anything like it in my entire life, and I was an altar boy. There were body-parts everywhere, some still on fire. I vomited several times, rendering any forensic evidence inadmissible in court, but like I said, we thought this was just a gas explosion. We weren't prepared to find this…" He held up a severed rabbit's head, waited a few moments for dramatic effect, and then lowered it again. "We're warning the people of Haddon to remain vigilant. This is the work of a very sick individual who may or may not already be in the city. Anyone seen carrying an axe in public should be treated with extreme caution. And if you're watching this, Mr Axe-Man, let it be known that we're coming for you. We will find you. And we will kill you."

"Ah, the old Liam Neeson," said Lou, turning the volume down on the TV set hanging on the wall. Its screen was smashed in three places, but that was how it was when he'd bought it.

Johnnie was speechless. "I'm speechless," he said, though he was clearly lying. "Pour me a drink will you, Lou. I've got a feeling today is going to be a bit of a clusterfuck."

*

"Lardies and Gentlemememen," Johnnie said, for his drink had turned into eight. "I am here…bef…fore you…as your ma…mer…mayo…" He sniggered. "I'm not…your…mayo, and you…you bloody good pe-people, are not…a sandwich." He sniggered again. The people standing in the church aisles were growing restless. This was demonstrated when a tin of tomatoes clobbered Mayor Ketchum on the side of the head. Luckily he was drunk, and so didn't feel it, but tomorrow there would be a great big lump. If only someone would throw a bag of frozen peas…

"What's going on, Johnnie!" said an irritated voice from the back of the room. "Should we be worries?"

LARRY II: THE SQUEEQUEL

"Should we be scared for the safety of our children?" added another.

"No m-more than-n ushual," said Johnnie. And then, twenty seconds after the fact: "Did shomeone throw a tin of t-tomatoesh at me?"

The Haddoners began to mutter amongst themselves. Words like 'madman' and 'serial killer' were banded about willy-nilly. It was chaos, and Mayor Ketchum was running out of ideas.

Just then, who else should jump up onto the pulpit but Lou, hands held out in a placatory fashion, reminding the crowd that this was a place of God, and it should be treated as such. The vagrant urinating at the side of the room zipped himself up and silently apologised, before making the sign of the cross – spectacles, testicles, wallet, and watch.

"People, people, people," said Lou, and Johnnie had never been so pleased to see a fella in all his life.

"I fu…fucking love you, Lou…" said the mayor to the newcomer (not to be confused with the actress and the bishop nor the bishop and the bishop's wife).

"What the mayor is trying to say," said Lou, "is that there is absolutely nothing to worry about.

We've had serial killers in our midst before, and none of us died then, did we?"

"But that was just Ed Gein," said an elderly woman at the front of the crowd. "And he was just passing through, doing a bit of furniture shopping."

"And did anyone become a part of his feng shui?" asked Lou. "Did any of your relatives get made into lampshades?" He waited, ignoring the hand that had just been thrust into the air at the back of the room. "So how is this any different?"

"That'sh what I wassss trying to say," added the mayor.

"No you weren't," whispered Lou conspiratorially. "For God's sake, man, pull yourself together. These people rely on you in a crisis."

"They…posshibly shouldn't," said Johnnie.

"So what you're saying," said one of the orange women from three pews back, "is that we just go about our business as usual and hope this sick fucker—" There were mumbles amongst the crowd, mainly from the devout lot, and the orange woman was quick to apologise. "—sorry, I forgot where I was for a moment there. This sick bleeping bleep of a bleep doesn't kill us while we bleeping bleep."

"Lady, I have no idea what you just said," said Lou. "But, yes, that's *exactly* what we have to do."

"And how will we know if we bump into this psycho?" asked the old lady at the front of the crowd.

The mayor laughed; the question itself wasn't funny. He just had a thing for old people. It was how they were all wrinkled up, like an old banknote. "I should th-think the axsh would be a d…dead giveaway."

"What the mayor is so indelicately trying to say," Said Lou, casting evils toward Johnnie, "is that you probably won't even realise you're looking at a maniac. Hell, he, or even she, could be in this church right now. You might be standing right next to our killer."

There were mutterings as those present checked the person next to them.

"It's very likely," Lou went on, "that whoever killed those people last night will ignore Haddon altogether. I mean, nobody likes Haddon, not even the people who live here. The bastard's probably halfway to Mexico by now, so what we need to do is continue as normal, and if you see anyone strange, contact the HDP."

"Couldn't herve put it m'better myshelf," the mayor said, waving his hands frantically about the place.

"What's he doing?" one of the orange ladies asked.

"Thinks it's Part Three," said another.

"Go on!" said the mayor. "Shoo. Begone. Getaway."

The crowd began to disperse, mumbling anxiously and filing out through the double-doors at the front of the church.

"That…that went well," slurred the mayor.

"You're an idiot," said Lou.

LARRY II: THE SQUEEQUEL

17
A Road (One of Many Surrounding Haddon)

Richard Goodnite was driving a stolen car around the edge of the city when he saw the man hobbling along the road, carrying a tattered suitcase which seemed to be held together by sheer willpower alone. Now Richard didn't normally stop for hitchhikers, especially when he was driving something hotter than a pair of nuddy women frolicking in a pepper patch, but there was something about this man's gait that got Richard right in the soft spot.

"Poor bastard," Richard said, turning down the stereo which had come free with the car (a bargain in itself). He slowed the car to a crawl, leaned across, and wound down the passenger-side window. "Hey, man, where you going?" said Richard. *If he's going to Haddon*, he thought, *I'll drop him just inside the city. If he's going anywhere else, I'll bid him good day, throw a couple of coins at him, and be on my joyriding way.*

"Is he talking to us?" said the man beneath the hood.

"I *am*," said Richard. "But who the devil are *you* talking to?" *He's old*, Richard thought. *Probably got a headful of dead relatives and war buddies.*

"Should I *kill* him?" said the man, still walking slowly beside the crawling car. "I am being quiet. Are you going to answer the fucking question, or am I going to have to punch you again?"

Now Richard, who knew a case of alzheimer's when he saw it, was really concerned for the man's safety. What if he was lost? What if the poor sonofabitch had put on his hoodie and packed his suitcase that very morning, left his home with every intention of returning, only to now find himself ambling along a busy road, miles away from home and not a bloody clue how to get back there?

"Are you lost, sir?" said Richard, for he'd been brought up to respect his elders. Steal their cars, by all means, but address them correctly should the need arise. "Are you a bit gone in the old brain, sir?"

The man punched himself in the face. There was a meaty crack as his balled fist connected with his snout.

"Don't do that, sir," Richard said, swerving to avoid a pothole. "You're going to do yourself a mischief. Why don't you hop in the car and we can figure out where you're going. The car's nicked, but you probably won't remember that long enough to grass me up to the HPD."

"The rules state," mumbled the man, still concealed by his hood, "that the body-count must be significantly higher than that of its predecessor, so why are you trying to talk me...yeah, I *appreciate* we're keeping a low profile, but...you know what? Take that." And he punched himself in the face again.

"East 17," said Richard. "Your go." It was a silly game, but he was willing to bite, at least until the poor guy regained his senses. Thirty seconds later, when it was clear the confused man had forgotten all about the game, Richard said, "It's getting warm out there, sir. Why don't you hop in the car and I'll take you to wherever it is you want to go."

The man stopped walking, so suddenly that Richard had to reverse a little. *This'll be a great story to tell Freddy later on*, he thought. *Picked up a mental hitcher, dropped him off at the hospital.* Oh, how they would laugh.

"Come on, sir, you know it makes sense."

"Makes sense," mumbled the man. He opened the car door and climbed in, placing his battered suitcase in the foot-well between his legs.

"Fuck, sir, you smell like someone took a shit

on your head," said Richard, for as respectful as he was to his elders, he was as honest as the next man when it came to funky stenches. "You don't work at the abattoir, do you?"

"That's right," said the man. "I don't work at the abattoir."

"Then what's with the bloody apron?" asked Richard. "You a butcher or something?"

"*Squeee*," said the man.

"Excuse me?"

"I said I *am* a butcher or something."

"Well which is it?"

"Which is what?"

"Are you a butcher or something?"

"I already *said* I was," said the man. "Are you going into Haddon?"

"In *this* car?" Richard said. "Not bloody likely. I can take you to the outskirts, if you like."

"How many outskirts does this city *have*?" asked the man. "I've been on the *outskirts* since I arrived. Can you drop me at the inskirts?"

"Haddon doesn't have any," said Richard as he pulled the car to the side of the road. "Only outskirts, and here we are."

"That was quick," said the man. "Thanks for the lift, and all that." He reached down and opened his suitcase.

"So I was *right*," said Richard as the man pulled out an axe. "You *are* a butcher or something."

"Or something," said the man, and buried the axe in Richard Goodnite's face.

*

Was that entirely necessary? asked the mask as Larry tied the dead kid's bandana around the lower half of his face. *I mean, he did give us a lift to the outskirts.*

"Fifty feet from where he picked us up," said Larry. "And anyway, he was asking too many questions." He climbed out of the car, wiped the bloody axe on the passenger seat and dropped it back into his suitcase. "Anyway, what did I say about it needing to be a higher body count?"

You said it needed to be a higher body count.

"Exactly," said Larry. "So with the massacre last night, about thirty people, add this one, makes…" Maths had never been his strong point.

Thirty-one, said the mask.

"Alright, smartarse," said Larry. "Look, there's a sign. It says…" Reading, like maths, had never been his strong point.

Welcome to Haddon, said the mask.

"Exactly. Welcome to Haddon," said Larry. "Which means we're on the outskirts, but as soon as we pass that sign, we'll be on the inskirts, and one step closer to finding that bitch and her boyfriend."

It was going to be a good day. He could smell it in the air.

LARRY II: THE SQUEEQUEL

18
The Mayor's Office

"What's that smell?" Amanda said.

"Sorry," said Sister Geoff. "Side-effect of the methadone, unfortunately. You're lucky my guts haven't dropped completely."

"Is somebody going to knock the fucking door," Freddy said, pinning his nostrils together.

Amanda knocked the door, and a lovely big door it was, too. So big was this door that Amanda's knock echoed. "What if he's opening new businesses this morning?" she said. "Ninety-nine percent of a mayor's job is cutting ribbons, did you know that?"

Sister Geoff, clearly not amused, hammered at the door with both fists. "Mayor Ketchum, open this door right now! I've got a party to go to this afternoon, you cun—"

The door slowly opened and there, with a bag of frozen peas pressed against the side of his head, stood Mayor Ketchum.

"What the fuck happened to you?" said the nun, barging past him and into the office. Amanda and Freddy followed in her slipstream.

"Had a little incident at the church," Johnnie

said.

"Dangerous places, churches," said Sister Geoff. "You wouldn't catch me in one, not on your nelly."

"What's all this about?" said the mayor.

"I'll *tell* you what it's about," said the nun. "It's about a masked madman coming to Haddon."

"Oh, *that*," said the mayor, slumping into his huge leather chair. "We don't even know if he's coming to Haddon."

"Oh, we do," said Freddy. "He's already here, or at least on the outskirts."

"And you are?" said the mayor, shaking his head and dropping the bag of frozen peas onto his desk. And a lovely big desk it was, too. So big was this desk that…well, you get the picture.

"Freddy Crowley," said Freddy. "And this is Amanda Bateman. And she's a rather sweary nun we're subcontracting some work out to."

The mayor frowned as he searched his memory for something just beyond his reach. Then his eyebrows arched, and he clicked his fingers three times. "*I* know you two," he said. "You were the idiots that went up to Camp Diamond Creek last year and almost got your asses handed to you by that lunatic in a pig-mask. What was his name again? Pigfuck? Hogface?—"

"Pigface," Amanda said.

"He *died* up there, didn't he? Only they didn't find any remains in the burnt debris, only the remains of those he'd slaughtered." The mayor opened his desk drawer – and what a lovely desk drawer it was, too – and pulled out a newspaper. There, right on the front page, was an artist's depiction of Larry 'Pigface' Travers. It wasn't very good as the artist had never had a go at a pig before, but the essentials were all there. The headline read: **Camp Crazy Slaughters Stereotypes, Burns to Death…Sequel Possible.**

"What does this have to do with anything?" said the mayor, for cottoning on to the obvious had never been his strong point. He was good at maths and reading, though.

"Pigface didn't die up at Diamond Creek," Amanda said, in that deadly serious way actresses do when explaining essential plot-points.

"What do you mean he didn't die up…the police report said there was an unmistakable smell of bacon in the air. It says right here in this article, a woman by the name of Betsy Krueger lopped off all his limbs, and then his head, before the cabin burned to the ground."

"That's all true," Freddy said. "But do you remember what happened over in Chicago with that ginger doll?"

"Who, Chucky?" said the mayor. "Of course I do. Never heard such nonsense in my entire life."

"It's not nonsense," Amanda said. "The little fucker kept coming back, no matter what happened to him, and we think the same thing is happening here."

Johnnie buried his face in his hands. "Oh, this is why you've got a nun, isn't it?" he said, voice muffled. "You think this Pigface character has come back from the dead." The derision in his voice was palpable.

"That's *exactly* what's going on," Freddy said. "And if we don't stop him, he's going to come down on this shitty city of yours like a ton of bricks." For dramatic effect, Freddy slammed both fists down on the desk. The mayor glowered at him for doing so, and he quickly peeled his hands away, apologising profusely.

"Look, kids, I don't know what you've been smoking or injecting, or if you've just got some sort of weird STD, but I find it hard to believe that a man who was dismembered and burnt to death a year ago has come back to life and is on his way to Haddon as we speak."

As if on cue, Amanda's eyes rolled back into her head. She made a low thrumming sound in her throat.

"What's the matter with her?" asked the mayor.

"I know. Fucking weird innit?" added Sister Geoff.

"Somehow, we don't know how, she's connected to Pigface's mind."

"What? Like Penn and Teller?" The mayor watched as Amanda swayed unsteadily back and forth.

"Who?" Freddy said.

"Couple of wankers from Vegas," said the mayor.

"Oh, well in that case, *nothing* like Penn and Teller. She's somehow tuned into him, as if part of his mind imprinted on hers when he reanimated."

"Assume I believe you for a minute," said the mayor, "and assume I'm not going to report all three of you to the police for partaking in illicit substances – I know Sister Geoff's got past form."

"I'm off it now," the nun said. "Apart from the weed, the methadone, the booze, and the miaow miaow, I'm as clean as a whistle." She looked ever so proud of herself, and rightfully so. No-one else in the room was.

"So let's say I believe that this madman, this *Pigface*, has returned from the grave and has decided to lay waste to our fair city—

"Bit of an exaggeration," Sister Geoff said. "It's a shithole."

"Stop interrupting when the mayor's trying to get to a point," Freddy said. He didn't care if the nun had his uncle's shotgun. She was liable to blow her own bollocks off trying to retrieve it from her tunic.

"What are we supposed to do about it?" the mayor finished. "And how long is she going to be like that?" he said, pointing at Amanda. "I've got a RadioShack to open in half an hour."

"She'll be out of it in a minute, hopefully with something we can use. You see, Mister Mayor—"

"Call me *Johnnie*."

"You see, Johnnie—"

"I've changed my mind," said the mayor. "Call me Mister Ketchum."

I'll call you a fucking ambulance in a minute, Freddy thought. "We're of the mind that Pigface's soul can be, what's the word…?"

"*Buggered*?" said the nun.

LARRY II: THE SQUEEQUEL

"Deported," Freddy said, "from its vessel. All we need to do is capture him, tie him up, and let Sister Geoff go to town on him with her Bible and whatnot."

"You're talking about an exorcism," said the mayor.

"If you want to put it like that," Freddy said.

"You might want to get your white-eyed friend checked out while you're at it." Johnnie motioned to Amanda, who was muttering something incomprehensible under her breath. "Splash a bit of holy water on the both of them."

Freddy hadn't thought about what would happen to Amanda once Pigface was out of the picture. What if, in killing the lunatic, part of Amanda died, too? What if she ended up cabbaged, like Stephen Hawking or that ginger one out of Girls Aloud? What if—

"Aye aye," the mayor said. "Looks like she's coming round. And not a moment too soon. Did I tell you I had a—"

"RadioShack to open in half an hour," said Sister Geoff. "Glad to see you've got your priorities in order, *Johnnie*." She added extra emphasis to his name, knowing full well it would royally piss him off.

"He's here," Amanda said, rubbing at her eyes as if a honeybee had just wanked polled all over her face. "He's in the city. I saw him walking toward…" She trailed off.

"Well this is awkward," said Sister Geoff, poking and prodding Amanda's arm. "I think she's had one too many vacancies."

"Will you stop bloody poking me?" Amanda said. "I was *thinking*."

"What did you see, Amanda?" Freddy said.

"Lights. Flashing lights. Lots of them. I couldn't make it out clearly through the eyeholes of his mask, but I think I've seen the place before."

"Where?" said Freddy.

"The arcade," Amanda said, and then with a bit more oomph. "The *arcade*! He's heading toward the *arcade*!"

"I guess he's heading toward the arcade," Sister Geoff said, pulling the mayor to his feet.

"Now hang on a jeffing *minute*," the mayor said. "I'm not chasing some masked maniac halfway around the city. That's what the police are for."

"Haven't you been listening to a damn word we've been *saying*?" Freddy said, surprised at the tone of his own voice. "The police can't stop him. At *best* they can slow him down. Without a nun,

LARRY II: THE SQUEEQUEL

they're *fucked*."

"I've never felt so wanted in my entire life," Sister Geoff said, winking at Freddy, who vomited a little in his mouth.

"You send *cops* after him, then…then you're going to be burying a lot of cops at the end of the week, and I'm pretty sure those big flags you drape over their coffins aren't cheap. Think about all the money you'll be saving."

The mayor considered her words. "Okay, but let it be known that I'm only doing it for the flags, and if the shit hits the fan, and you kids end up with your heads on backwards or not on at all, then I won't be held responsible."

"Fair enough," Amanda said. "Now can we get over to Armand's before it's too late?"

But part of her knew it already would be.

19
Armand's Arcade

Larry stepped in off the street and glanced about the place. Everywhere he looked there were flashing lights. It was a good job he wasn't epileptic; he'd have been on the carpet, doing the worm-dance. Music, loud and distracting, assaulted him from all directions. Every now and then, an 8-bit bleep would surprise him. As a child of the woods, he had never seen such craziness, such garishness, such unadulterated *filth*. Young people stood in front of flashing machines, bashing at buttons with both hands. In the middle of the room, a pair of kids bashed a disc back and forth with hovercraft paddles. Beyond them, a man sat in a wire cage, as if he was afraid of being pelted with bottles.

She's not here, said the mask. *We'd be better off…what are you doing?*

"What does it look like I'm doing?" Larry said.

It looks like you're taking your axe out, said the mask.

"It does, doesn't it?"

Put it away before somebody sees it, said the mask.

"I *want* them to see it," said Larry, placing his

suitcase against the wall. "Not only do I want them to see it, but I want them to *feel* it."

How is that keeping a low profile? asked the mask.

"It really isn't," Larry replied. "I'm a slasher, not some clandestine serial killer. Slashers don't concern themselves with such things a low profiles. When that big bastard with the hockey mask took Manhattan a few years back, did he sneak around in the shadows, keeping a low profile? No, because he was a slasher, and slashers don't particularly care if they're spotted out in the wild."

"Excuse me," echoed a voice. It seemed to come from all around. It took Larry a few moments to realise the voice belonged to the man in the cage, who was speaking into some sort of plastic handset. "No axes allowed. If you want to come and play the machines, you're going to have to leave your axe at the door."

We should go, the mask opined.

All eyes were now on Larry, though only briefly. These kids were too caught up in their videogames to care if someone had an axe.

"Buddy, I'm not going to tell you twice," said the man behind the wire mesh. "You either leave the axe at the door, or you find another arcade to break the rules in.

Larry reached up and removed the hood and scarf which had been concealing his face. His grin was so broad, it met somewhere at the back of his head.

"Jeeeeeesus Ch...what the fuck is *wrong* with you, bro?" said the caged man, clearly perturbed by this new development. It was almost as if he'd never seen a maniac in a pig mask wielding an axe before.

Oh dear, said the mask.

"*Squeeeeeeeeeeeeeeeee!*" said Larry. He hobbled forward a few feet, bringing the axe down on some kid in a baseball cap. As the kid's head split in two, the words **GAME OVER** flashed up on the screen in front of him, proving once again that synchronicity was everywhere.

Larry pulled the axe out and swung back toward the door, where a set of identical twins (or a glitch in the Matrix) were making good their escape. As soon as they realised their path was blocked, they cowered back against the wall.

"Don't kill us," said the one on the left.

"*Please!*" gasped the one on the right.

"We've got so much to *give!*" they said in unison, and that was the straw that broke the

LARRY II: THE SQUEEQUEL

camel's back, for there was nothing more terrifying than identical twins. Larry swung the axe down, embedding it in the plastered wall. The doppelgangers looked up at it, fear in their eyes, and were still looking at it when Larry grabbed their heads in his huge hands and slammed them together as hard as he could. Eyes and teeth flew everywhere. For fuck's sake, they even *gargled* in harmony...

A loud bang echoed about the place, and Larry's right shoulder seemed to explode. He released the twins' heads and they slumped to the ground. Turning, he quickly realised where the bang had come from. Standing there, out of his cage, was the man, the proprietor, Armand – though Larry didn't know that. In his tremulous hands he held a shotgun; its barrels smoking. He looked terribly nervous, did Armand.

"Don't you move, asshole," said Armand. "The cops are on their way."

See, said the mask. *This is why low profiles exist, and if I remember correctly, it didn't end terribly well for the hockey-mask guy over in Manhattan, and you're hardly him, are you? I mean, you're twice as old as he was—*

"I don't think age matters once you're dead," said Larry. "Anyway, shut up for a minute. Things are about to get very interesting."

"Who the fuck are you *talking* to, man?" Armand said, scanning the surrounding area. He saw kids – his *customers* – cowering everywhere he looked, and he wanted to tell them all to run away as fast as they could, but he had control of the situation now, and it wasn't good business telling your punters to scarper, especially when you had the upper hand. "And who the fuck do you think you *are*, coming in here and chopping up my clientele?" He pulled the trigger again. Larry's left shoulder exploded in a cloud of blood and bone, but he was pleasantly surprised to find that it didn't hurt, not at all, not even a little sting, *nosiree…*

The man, Armand, must have been expecting Larry to drop to his knees, to start begging for mercy, and please, whatever you do, tell the police he was remorseful for what he had done. When none of that happened, Armand's expression dropped like a lead balloon, and he began fumbling nervously into his pocket, no doubt to replenish the spent shells in his shotgun. "You're not r-right, man," said Armand, walking slowly backwards but keeping the useless shotgun trained on Larry.

Whatever gave him that idea? said the mask. *Will*

LARRY II: THE SQUEEQUEL

you just finish him so we can get the fuck out of here? I don't hear sirens, but that doesn't mean the pigs…sorry, the cops aren't on their way…

Larry turned and pulled his axe from the wall. Plaster rained down on the squashed twins below. Armand was still trying to load his shotgun when Larry threw the axe. There was a meaty thump as the blade embedded in Armand's chest, and then he was flying backwards, his face contorted with shock, wondering how very strange it was that a day which had started off okay had taken a remarkable turn for the worse. He clattered against the cage and slumped to the carpet, blood spewing slowly from the wide gash in his chest.

The kids hiding behind pool tables and arcade machines collectively inhaled. Their hero was dead, butchered in the most beastly manner. At least three of them, however, were already eyeing up the position, and would – should they survive the next few minutes – pop off home and begin work on their CVs.

In the distance, sirens wailed.

That sound means we have to go now, said the mask.

Larry walked slowly across the room, retrieved his axe from the proprietor's still-twitching corpse, before leaving the arcade in a much worse state than when he'd arrived.

A minute later, three cowering boys stood up and rushed out through the open doors.

"My job!" one of them said.

"Not on your nelly!" said another.

"—" said the third, for he was far more sensitive to insane amounts of violence than the other two; the previous few minutes had been somewhat traumatising and had rendered the poor bastard dumb.

*

"Well *this* isn't a good sign," said Freddy as they arrived at Armand's. Police cars were scattered about the place; cops were standing around talking to witnesses and passers-by; a parking attendant was surreptitiously ticketing the cop cars, for he needed the bonus at the end of the month, and, well, as far as he was concerned it should be the same rules for everyone.

The arcade itself was cordoned off due to the horrific scene within, though no-one *knew* there was a horrific scene within because it was cordoned off. Luckily, the investigating officers had investigated the horrific scene within before they had cordoned the place off, or they too would have been none the wiser as to what was happening, or why they had been called out in the first place.

"Aw, it's cordoned off," said Sister Geoff. "I was hoping to have a few goes on Anders Breivik's Day Off."

A pair of detectives, whose names both ended in –wallowicz, appeared in front of the mayor.

"What are you doing here, Mister Mayor?" said Detective Bobwallowicz. "Don't you have premises to open?"

Detective Billwallowicz sniggered. "Yeah, Mister Mayor. Oh, by the way, that over there is crime scene tape, designed to cordon off premises in which horrific scenes have occurred. We'd be really grateful if you didn't try cutting it."

Bobwallowicz snorted. "Good one," he said, patting his partner on the back.

"Are these guys for real?" Freddy said.

"What happened here?" asked the mayor.

"Erm, horrific events," said Bobwallowicz, sounding more like a petulant child than a detective of the HPD. "Duh."

Sister Geoff had had enough, and barged the mayor aside. "Listen, you pair of cunts," she said, poking each of them in the shoulder. "I've got a party to be at in four hours' time and you cockwombles really aren't helping, so why don't you just tell Mayor Ketchum what's happened here, and we'll be out of your hair."

The Wallowiczes were flummoxed. Never before had they been reprimanded by a nun, and it didn't feel nice, no, not at all. Nuns were supposed to be nice, gentle, and good with children – unlike their male counterparts – but this one was crude, rough around the edges, and not even the worst parent in the world would leave her in charge of their kids.

Bobwallowicz cleared his throat. "Apparently, some psycho in a pig mask decided to kill Armand and a bunch of kids."

"*See*," said the nun. "That wasn't too difficult, now, was it?"

"Not at all," said Bobwallowicz.

"We were too late," Amanda said, stifling the tears which threatened to make an appearance any moment. "Those poor children."

"Poor Armand," Freddy said. Then he remembered Armand ejecting him and Rich from the arcade the previous day, and thought, *Serves him right*.

Billwallowicz, now frowning, pulled a notepad from his breast pocket. "Who are you, anyway?"

he said. "Do you have any information about what might have happened here?"

"Yeah, I reckon some psycho in a pig mask decided to kill Armand and a bunch of kids," said the nun, sarcastically. "You can quote me on that, if you like."

"We might know who is responsible—" the mayor began, but Amanda interrupted.

"For the 9/11 attacks," she said.

Bobwallowicz and Billwallowicz exchanged a look. The kind of look that suggested they believed they were dealing with a whack-job.

"Al-Qaeda?" said Bobwallowicz, scratching his bald head.

"Oh, you already *know*," Amanda said. "Well, in that case our work here is done. Have a pleasant day, detectives, and I'd keep that Al-Qaeda info to yourself. You never know who you can trust." She walked away from the Wallowiczes; Freddy, Sister Geoff, and Mayor Ketchum quickly followed.

"What was that all about?" said the mayor. "We know who killed those people, and it sure as hell had nothing to do with Al-Qaeda."

"You want to tell them that Pigface, a reanimated maniac seeking retribution for his own death, is responsible for this?" Amanda whispered, for the Wallowiczes were still lurking in the vicinity. "There's not a fat lot we can do to stop that bastard from Haddon Asylum, is there?"

"She's right," Freddy said. "And there's no point putting more lives on the line."

"Pity you weren't thinking like that when you phoned the shagging nunnery," Sister Geoff said.

"So what do we do *now*?" asked the mayor. "Don't tell me we have to wait for old White Eyes here to have another vision?"

"We have to wait for old White—"

"Thought as much," said the mayor, glancing at his watch. It was a nice watch. Very gold. Pinched his arm-hairs every now and then, but that was a small price to pay for such a nice, very gold watch.

"That's a nice watch," said the nun, wandering whether he would miss it if it wasn't there.

"Thanks," said the mayor. "It pinches my arm-hairs every now and then, but that's a small price to pay for such a nice, very gold watch."

"Can I have it?"

"No you can't," said the mayor.

"Shame," said the nun. "I don't have as much arm-hair as you."

"Look, I've got to go and open this

LARRY II: THE SQUEEQUEL

RadioShack," said the mayor. "I'd appreciate it if you tagged along, since you seem to know more about this Pigface character than anyone else."

"Will there be cake?" asked Sister Geoff.

"No."

"Drugs?"

"I can have you put in a cell, you know."

And so Amanda, Freddy, and Sister Geoff followed Mayor Ketchum halfway across town, to where a ribbon, a pair of scissors, and a crowd of twelve anxiously awaited his arrival.

Adam Millard

20
Tan Yo Hide

The name of the orange lady in charge was Chrystal (of *course* it bloody was) and she hadn't always been orange. As a child she had been a regular porcelain, and as a teenager she was comfortable wearing an off-bisque shade. In fact, it wasn't until she turned thirty that she opted to go that extra step, thus becoming the walking-talking-crinklier-than-a-leather-handbag-cheesy-poof that she was today. Still, as far as she was concerned, she was absolutely gorgeous, and don't you try to tell her otherwise.

Today was a very special day for Tan Yo Hide. Only that morning, Chrystal had received a phone-call from a VIP. None other than Same Treat, in fact. The following is a transcription of that particular call.

Chrystal: *Hello? Tan Yo Hide, Chrystal speaking, how may I help you?*
Sam Treat: *I woke up this morning looking like death. I mean, I could make the Queen of England look like Queen Latifah, right now, and I've got a very important party to attend this afternoon. Can you make me brown?*

LARRY II: THE SQUEEQUEL

Chrystal: *I can make you orange.*
Sam Treat: *What about mocha? Can you do mocha?*
Chrystal: *I can do orange.*
Sam Treat (sighing): *Darling, this is Sam Treat, supermodel extraordinaire, legs up to my armpits, one boob marginally larger than the other. Can you do mocha?*
Chrystal: *OhmyGod! Miss Treat, How wonderful it is to hear from you.*
Sam Treat: *Of course it is. Now, about my tan.*
Chrystal: *We can do mocha, we can do walnut, caramel, tawny, off-faeces. We can do honey, marigold, apricot. We can do Kardashian, rust, amber, kidney-stone—*
Sam Treat: *Mocha is fine.*
Chrystal (clearly excited): *When can we expect you! The girls won't believe…hang on a sec…Debbie! Debbie! Guess who I'm talking to right now! Go on, have a guess! Brad Pitt, she says. No, have another guess. Joe Biden? Who the f— have another go.*
Sam Treat: *Beeeeeeeeeeeeeeeeeep*
Chrystal: *Miss Treat? Are you there? Oh, she's gone. It was Sam Treat, Debs. You know, the supermodel with the legs up to her armpits and one boob marginally smaller than the other? She's coming in for a Mocha. Can you believe that? Sam Treat, coming here for a spray? Why am I still holding this phone? Honestly, sometimes I—* [Call Terminated]

Needless to say, Chrystal was thrilled at the prospect of a celebrity in her salon. She'd put on a bit of a spread – ham sandwiches, pork scratchings, bacon vol-au-vents, the usual fare – and had given the booth a once over with Lemon Pledge. Her assistant for the day, Debbie Lee-Ray, was equally as excited, and had got herself all dolled up for the occasion. So there they were, a pair of orange ladies wearing shades of bright green and red, waiting for the beautiful Sam Treat to arrive at *Tan Yo Hide*.

"What if *he* got her?" said Chrystal, glancing down at her watch. It was a nice watch. Orange, covered in spray-tan, but apart from that it did its job.

"Who?" Debbie said, shoving a bacon vol-au-vent into her mouth and frantically chewing.

"Miss *Treat*," said Chrystal.

"I know *that*," said Debbie. "I meant *who*? As in, what if *who* got Miss Treat?"

"I don't know. That's why I was asking you."

"No…oh, deary, deary me, this is confusing. We both know that we're talking about Miss Treat, right?"

"Right."

LARRY II: THE SQUEEQUEL

"So *who* would refer to the person to which you are eluding, the one who may or may not have got Miss Treat, correct?"

"I don't know," said Chrystal. "But what if he *has* got her? What if he's killed her or kidnapped her or—"

"*Who?*"

"Miss *Treat!* Honestly, sometimes I wonder why I even bother talking to you."

Just then, the door swung open and in walked Sam Treat, flanked by what appeared to be a moose of some kind, thusly rendering the last few lines of dialogue completely unnecessary.

"Ah, Miss Treat," Chrystal said, jumping up and down on the spot. "You have no idea how *thrilled* we are that you chose *Tan Yo Hide* to turn you a nice shade of mocha."

"As you can see," added Debbie, motioning to the fine spread they'd put on for their VIP, "we've put on a bit of food for you. Hope you're not allergic to swine—"

"Actually, I'm vegetarian," said Sam, removing her shoes.

"Well, that's knackered that, then," Chrystal said. "The thought was there, though. Maybe we could rustle you up a quiche? Perhaps an omelette?

Debbie works wonders with crepes, don't you Debs?"

"Actually, I ate three days ago," said Sam. "Didn't I, Martha?"

Martha, who wasn't a moose after all but a very tricky-looking woman, flipped through a notebook. "That's right," she said, running her finger down the page. "You had a Caesar salad on Tuesday, followed by three croutons and seventeen glasses of Chardonnay."

"It was the croutons that did it," Sam said, patting her tiny tummy. A hollow sound echoed around the tiny salon. "So where do you want us?"

"Us?" said Chrystal. "You're going to have your pet done as well?"

"Do you *mind*?" Martha said, exasperated.

"She didn't mean anything by it," said Debbie. "Just that the spray doesn't work well with excess fur."

"I'll sit this one out," said Martha.

"Probably for the best," concurred Sam. "Remember that time you had your crack waxed?"

Martha nodded, solemnly.

"Three days we were in there," said Sam. "They had enough hair to stuff a dozen cushions."

"I really don't—"

LARRY II: THE SQUEEQUEL

"No of *course* you don't," Sam said. "And why would you? It's absolutely disgusting." She turned to the orange ladies. "Let's get this show on the road, shall we? Got a very important party to attend in a couple of hours."

"Walk this way," said Chrystal, before waddling into a back room.

Sam and Martha waddled after her, although it felt a little unnatural.

Debbie forced three sausage-rolls into her mouth and rolled her eyes.

*

Fifteen minutes later, they were all standing around the mini-buffet once again, only now Sam Treat was standing in front of a mirror with a towel around her extremities, screaming at the top of her lungs while her assistant frantically fanned her with her notebooks.

"I can assure you, Miss Treat, that it will calm down!" said Chrystal.

"I asked for fucking mocha!" said the supermodel. "This is a tangerine tan, if I ever I saw one!"

"It will be mocha in a few weeks," said Chrystal. "Oh, deary me, this has gone terribly wrong, hasn't it?"

"No shit!" gasped Sam. "Now I've got to rock up at Harry Hunter's party looking like a Circus Peanut in a Hazmat suit!"

"I'm sure Mister Hunter won't notice," said Chrystal. Debbie had taken to rearranging the food on the table into alphabetic order.

"Won't notice?" said Sam, exposing herself to her reflection. One boob was certainly smaller than the other, or was that larger than; either way she looked a little skewiff. "I'll be the only one there glowing in the dark!"

"Colourful is always good," assured Chrystal. "It won't look half as bad by the time you get there. You're just not used to it yet."

"Oh, I'm used to it," said Sam, haughtily covering herself over once more. "I'm pretty sure my lawyer will be intrigued about it, too. How long have you been operating for?"

"A day," said Debbie, through a mouthful of bacon.

"Well, I hope you enjoyed yourselves," Sam said, dropping the towel and climbing into her clothes. Getting dressed is so much more difficult when you're angry, which was why Sam Treat found herself with a head in an armhole, a leg in a headhole, and the rest of her all knotted up like a

LARRY II: THE SQUEEQUEL

knob of ginger.

Martha, the assistant, assisted, and it wasn't long before everything was in the correct order.

"Don't think you've heard the end of this," said Sam, before turning and storming out, her moose in tow.

"There goes another happy customer," said Debbie.

"Shut up, Debs," said Chrystal. "Just shut up."

*

You hear that racket? said the mask. *All those sirens and whatnot?*

Larry nodded, for he *did* hear them. There were an awful lot of them, dopplering through the streets. It was as if they had nothing better to do. "Somebody must have done something naughty."

And do you think that might be you? asked the mask.

"I bloody hope not," Larry said. "Sounds like they've got ever cop in the city out looking for this perp."

Better find somewhere to lay low for a while, said the mask. *And I don't know about you, but I'm friggin' starving here...*

"You're a mask," said Larry. "How is that even possible?"

I'm part of you, you buffoon. If you're hungry, I'm hungry.

"Now that you mention it," Larry said, rubbing at his considerable belly, "I could murder some food."

Let's just find something that's already dead, shall we? said the mask. *And where the hell are we, anyway?*

Larry stopped momentarily, took in his surroundings. "I'm going to go out on a limb and say that we're by a load of industrial trashcans," he said, for they were indeed by a load of industrial trashcans. There were doors all along one side of the…well, it wasn't quite a street. More of a back-passage. The kind of back-passage it was easy to get lost in. As back-passages went, this one was relatively clean. Larry had seen some dirty back-passages in his lifetime, but this one was well looked after.

Just then, and not a moment too soon as far as the anti-back-passage-jokes-brigade were concerned, a figure emerged from one of the backdoors, trash in hand, fag in mouth, and proceeded to dispose of said trash in its proper receptacle.

Larry froze, watching as the woman – who was incredibly orange, Larry thought – got rid of her

LARRY II: THE SQUEEQUEL

rubbish before disappearing in through the backdoor. This backdoor was filthy, and Larry had seen a lot of filthy—

She was a bit orange, wasn't she? said the mask. *And leathery, like one of those cheap handbags you can buy at the airport…*

"I was thinking the same thing," said Larry, and of course he was, even though he wasn't sure what an airport was. "And the *state* of that backdoor—"

The approaching sirens drowned out his words, which was just as well. *We need to get out of this back-passage,* said the mask. *This will be the first place the cops think to search for us. They always rummage around in back-passages when they're looking for someone.*

"And go *where?*" said Larry. "We appear to be trapped in this back-passage. In fact, I can't remember how we even got here."

Head for that filthy backdoor, said the mask.

And so Larry did just that.

*

"Can you believe how rude she was?" Chrystal said as she re-entered the salon. Debbie nodded. "Well, I shan't be buying anything that bitch endorses ever again." *Apart from the double-wear foundation and the eyeliner,* she thought. *Oh, and the tampons, and maybe the leg-waxing strips… but apart from that…*

"Celebrities are all the same," said Debbie, moving into the kitchen area of the salon. Chrystal was in the next room, cleaning down a massage table. "You remember that time Prince Charles popped by for a colonic irrigation, then spent the entire time complaining about how cold your hands were?"

"That's royalty for you, though," Chrystal shouted back. "He was alright after I sat on them for ten minutes."

"Yeah, but he refused to sign the guestbook," said Debbie as she put the kettle on. She dropped teabags into cups. "I think it was because you told him he'd never be King."

"I thought he already *knew* that," said Chrystal. "Barring an absolute fucking tragedy, he's got no chance, and I told him as much."

"*'I'm more likely to sit in that throne than you,'* you told him. And if I remember correctly, you offended his missus."

"*Well*," said Chrystal. "She's no Diana, is she?"

"*'Face like Rod Hull taking a shit'* was what you said," said Debbie.

"And I stand by it," said Chrystal.

Debbie, still waiting for the kettle to boil, rattled her fingers on the worktop. She was about to fetch the milk from the fridge when she swore she heard heavy breathing.

"Is that you?" she called.

"Is *what* me?" replied Chrystal.

"Breathing heavy. Sounds like Darth Vader having a wank?"

"Not me," she said. "I can't hear anything."

But Debbie could, and it appeared to be coming from the cupboard at the far end of the kitchen, next to the back door, which was wide open.

"You left the back door wide open," Debbie said.

"Did I?" said Chrystal. "I swore I shut it. Maybe the wind blew it open."

There wasn't a breath of wind outside, and that didn't explain the heavy breathing emanating from the cupboard. "Chrystal, can you come in here for a minute?" said Debbie, nervously staring toward the cupboard.

"I'd rather not," said Chrystal. "Especially if there's someone hiding in the cupboard, heavy breathing. Remember what the mayor said at that meeting?"

"Something about us not being sandwiches," said Debbie as she moved slowly toward the cupboard. "I wasn't really paying attention."

"He said to remain vigilant," said Chrystal. "And what better way to remain vigilant than by ignoring strange sounds coming from cupboards, at least until they go away."

Debbie, however, couldn't ignore it. There was someone in there – having a stroke, perhaps, or several by the sounds of it. "Hello?" she said. "Who's in the cupboard?"

"You can't ask who's in the cupboard," Chrystal said from the adjacent room. "You've got to build up to it. Start with 'Is anyone there?' and work your way up."

"Is anyone—"

"Yes," came the response from the cupboard. "There is most definitely someone here." And then, under its breath, the voice said, "Well, she asked, didn't she? What was I supposed to do? Ignore her? Pretend that we're not here? For fuck's sake, I can't win with you, can I, you—"

"Animal, vegetable, or mineral?" said Debbie.

"What?" asked the voice. "What kind of a question is that? How many talking minerals do you know?"

"Animal, vegetable, *mineral?*" Debbie said, more insistent this time.

LARRY II: THE SQUEEQUEL

"For crying out...*animal*," said the voice.

"Ask him whether he's a celebrity?" Chrystal said, appearing in the kitchen doorway with a chamois leather in one hand a half-eaten sausage roll in the other.

"Are you a celebrity?" Debbie said, though quite why a celebrity would be hiding in their kitchen cupboard was beyond her.

"Depends," came the reply. "Am I well-known? Yes. Do I pose for photographs and hang around swanky nightclubs letting pretty girls lick my neck? Not on your nelly."

"Ooh," said Chrystal, forcing the rest of the sausage-roll into her orange face. "This is tricky."

"Why are you hiding in our cupboard?" Debbie said.

"—" said the voice, followed by, "—"

"'—' is not an acceptable answer," said Chrystal. In the background, sirens grew louder.

"Sorry," said the voice. "I'm a mass murder/slasher and I'm lying low for a moment, just until those sirens piss off."

"Oh," said Chrystal.

"Oh," concurred Debbie, taking small steps away from the cupboard. "We'll leave you to it, then."

The door flew open, so hard that it splintered in its frame. Standing there, between shelves lined with food, waxing-strips, scented oils, and a million canned shades of undiluted orange, was a man in a pig mask. The axe in his right hand looked sharp enough to do some real damage; the tin of pork luncheon meat in his other hand looked only slightly less threatening. The man in the mask was reading the back of the tin, as if trying to tot up its calorie content. After a few seconds, he slowly looked in the direction of the gobsmacked orange ladies, one of which was still chewing frantically on a sausage-roll.

"Like *pig* meat, do we?" he said.

"You're *him*!" gasped Debbie. "You're the one who butchered all those people last night!"

The killer dropped the tin of luncheon meat and straightened up, for he was a little hunched over, almost like a question mark. His back audibly cracked. "Got a body-count to think of," he said. "This is a sequel, after all."

Chrystal began to wave the leather chamois about the place.

"It's Part Two," said the killer.

"Oh," said Chrystal, and lowered the rag.

"Shouldn't we be running away?" said Debbie,

calm as you like.

"Are we major characters?" said Chrystal.

"We've been in it for a bit," said Debbie.

"Yeah, but have we done anything to alter the course of the plot?"

"Probably not."

"Then I don't think running is going to do us much good."

"I don't know," said the killer. "I quite like the thrill of the chase, and all that bollocks. I'll even give you a three second head-start." He glanced at his watch. It wasn't a man's watch; in fact, it wasn't a watch at all, but if he had a watch, that's definitely where he would keep it. "Starting…now!"

The orange women turned and rushed for the door as fast as their not-so-little orange legs could carry them. Behind them, the killer yelled, "Squeeeeee!" which meant that their three seconds were up. As those lovely Fugees once sang: *Ready or not, here I come.*

Chrystal and Debbie were only halfway across the salon – next to the ironic buffet, to be exact – when Debbie pulled up and turned to her colleague. "Is there something in my back? Feels like there's something in my back."

Chrystal turned her co-worker around and

hissed. "You've got an axe in your back," she said. "Fuck me, Debs, that's got to hurt."

"Like nothing I've experienced before," said Debbie. "And I went to a Catholic school." She spun around and around, like a dog chasing its tail, trying to reach the axe handle.

"Keep still," Chrystal said. "I've got it." She placed one knee at the base of Debbie's spine, grabbed onto the handle, and pulled the axe free. Blood geysered into her face, turning her satsuma tan into a crimson mess. It didn't matter, for she had the axe now, and though Debbie looked buggered—

"Can I have my axe back," said the killer, holding out his hand expectantly.

"Since you asked so nicely," Chrystal said, and held out the axe before snatching it back just before the killer could latch onto it. "What the hell am I thinking? No, you *can't* have it. You're only going to kill us with it. Look at what you've done to Debs. She hasn't been that white since she was eight, have you Debs?"

"There was that Goth convention in 2009," Debbie said through a mouthful of blood. "I feel ever so woozy." As if to demonstrate just how woozy she felt, she fell face-down onto the buffet-

LARRY II: THE SQUEEQUEL

table, sending sausage-rolls and vol-au-vents into the air. When the pork products settled – it took a while, for sausage-rolls aren't called sausage-stays for a reason – Chrystal glanced down at her dead colleague and sighed.

"Un-be-fucking-lievable. Do you have any idea how hard it is to find decent, hard-working orange people?"

"Willy Wonka didn't have a problem," said the killer, snatching the axe from the irate woman. Her mouth fell open in a terrified O. She looked like a sex-doll, if sex-dolls had fake tans.

Chrystal turned and, well, made it one step closer to the door before her head came off. The killer *Squeeeeeeeeed!* and Chrystal would have screamed if she'd been able to, but the fact of the matter is, and I believe it was Nietzsche who said it first, *You can't scream for shit if you don't have your vocal cords,* or something like that…

The head thumped against the far wall, toppling a Channing Tatum calendar (2013 – a vintage year for Channing fans everywhere), before landing in a waste-paper basket, as severed heads are wont to do.

Outside, the sirens howled through the streets, but at least they were howling in the right direction. That is to say they were going away, rather than the alternative.

Why do people do that to themselves? asked the mask.

"What?" said Larry. "Decapitate themselves with an axe?" As far as he was concerned, people tended *not* to do that to themselves. Something about getting the swing right. Of course, you could always rig up a whatchamacallit, let a machine do the severing, so to speak, but that takes knowledge in engineering, and the kind of people that want to lop off their own heads with an axe are not likely to be possessed of such ingenuity.

Make themselves orange, said the mask, which made more sense. *I just don't see the appeal.*

Larry wiped the bloody axe-blade on his apron. "Haven't the foggiest," he said. "Would it be cannibalism if I noshed a cocktail sausage?"

LARRY II: THE SQUEEQUEL

21
RadioShack

Elegant Victorian buildings lined the street, replete with detailed fretwork, ornamental brickwork, terracotta panelling, stunning swirls, volutes, and so on. Each building had its own beautiful style, from the vernacular to the Italianate. Pity, then, that the whole thing was buggered over by satellite dishes and graffiti, not to mention shuttered shops and boarded-up soup-kitchens.

"Haddoners, friends, and people who are just here for the free food," began the mayor, whose headache was starting to play merry hell with his facial features. "We are gathered here today, on Neve Campbell Street, to witness the birth of yet another RadioShack, because, let's be honest, where else are we going to be able to buy miniature lightbulbs from?"

"Fry's Electronics!" yelled John Fry from the circle-pit. "Home of Fast, Friendly, Courteous Service. Your Best Buys are always at Fry's!"

Someone – a man possessed by the demon of Charles D. Tandy – donked John Fry on the head with a cricket bat and carried him off to an awaiting ambulance, where he would be resuscitated at a later date, or not at all.

"It brings me great joy," continued the mayor, "to pronounce this RadioShack open to the general public." And with that, he cut the ribbon stretching across the store's doorway, and fifty potential customers turned around and went home.

"Can we go now?" Amanda said. "You sure you haven't got a Wendy's to open, or a Krispy Kreme to bless, or a Best Buy to throw eggs at?" Her sarcasm was duly noted, though not by Mayor Johnnie Ketchum, who just didn't get sarcasm at the best of times.

"Not this week," said the mayor. "So what's the plan? Any more visions?"

Amanda shook her head. "Not for a while, but we need to put our thinking caps on."

Freddy did just that. "Wait, I'm not wearing mine if none of you are going to bother." He took it off, scrunched it up, and thrust it back whence it came.

"You're a killer," said Amanda.

"No I'm not," said the mayor.

"Hypothetically, you're a killer—"

"Who told you that?" said the mayor. "Have you been talking to my ex-wife? Because what happened with Tiggles wasn't my fault. It was the lawnmower…it…it got away from me."

"No, I'm trying to put you into Pigface's shoes," said Amanda.

"I'm a nine-and-a-quarter," said the mayor.

"Would anyone take offence if I punched the mayor on the snotter?" asked Sister Geoff, balling her fists. Her knuckle-tattoos really stood out in this light.

"Hypothetically, you're a killer," Amanda went on, "and you're new in town. Hungry for blood, and yet trying to keep a low profile, where do you go?"

"Probably to a shoe-shop," said the mayor. "For some nine-and-a-quarters."

Freddy held the nun back by her habit. "Can we take this seriously," said he. "There are lives at stake."

"If I was him," said the mayor, "I'd probably go to the busiest place in the city. Slashers don't tend to keep a low profile. At least, that hockey guy over in Manhattan never worried about it."

"He's right," Amanda said. "Pigface won't give a shit if he's spotted, especially if he's semi-immortal. So where's the busiest place in the city on a Thursday afternoon?"

The mayor turned to Freddy, and Freddy turned to the nun, and the nun lit a tailor made, because this whole thing was more stress than it was worth.

"You mentioned something about a party?" Amanda said to Sister Geoff.

The nun shrugged. "Which I'm going to be late for, at this rate."

"What party?" asked the mayor.

"Fuck," said Freddy. "That's where he'll go."

And Sister Geoff frowned. "Well, bugger me," she said.

"If you think it will help," said the mayor.

"He's going to Harry Hunter's," said the nun.

"How quickly can we get there?" said Amanda.

"Half-an-hour," said Sister Geoff, checking her watch. It wasn't a man's watch, unless said man was a big fan of Mother Teresa's wizened face. The big hand was pointing at her forehead, while the little hand was hovering just shy of her right eye. Sister Geoff knew what that meant. "It's two o'clock. The party starts any time now, if it hasn't already."

"We need to hurry the fuck up," said Freddy.

And hurry the fuck up they did, which was why, fifteen minutes later, they were standing at a bus-stop, tapping their respective feet and praying

LARRY II: THE SQUEEQUEL

to God they weren't going to be too late.

22
Harry Hunter's Mansion

There are no two ways about it; porn is a huge industry. With more than $15bn in revenue generated annually, it's on a par with Hollywood's box office and the amount of cocaine snorted at a Lindsay Lohan bash. You don't need to be a great actor to star in porn…you just need to be *there*, and with at least one piece of genitalia, not necessarily in the right order. One of the greatest pornstars of the last twenty years, Ivana Bucketflaps, had nary an acting credit to her name when she made her first film, *Breakfast in Tiffany*. By the time her hundredth film was released (and what a corker *In Diana Jones: The Temple of Poon* was!) she had more money in the bank than the First Lady – not Eve, the other one. By the time her thousandth film came out – *Up Her Majesty's Secret Cervix*, by which point she was starting to get a little bit sore – she was richer than Oprah, Gina Rinehart, and the woman who does the voices in *Fifi and the Flowertots* combined. Within a quarter of a century, she had gone from strip-bar dancer to multi-billionaire, and along the way she had fallen in love.

With Harry Hunter.

LARRY II: THE SQUEEQUEL

To fans of porn (not me, I just work here), Harry Hunter is a God. A seventy-year old man with a forty-year-old ex-pornstar wife, Harry's had his fair share of Notorious VAG. He was one of the first producers to combine shemales with transsexuals, confusing porn fans worldwide. There is not a sexual position on earth that Harry hasn't seen. In fact, over the years he's discovered at least fifty new ones, put them all in a nice book (laminated, of course) and sold it to the mass-market, because if Harry Hunter knows anything about porn, it's that people will buy anything if it means emptying their sacks.

His mansion was testament to just how well he and Ivana had done over the years. With more staircases than your average staircase convention, The Hunter Mansion was the kind of building gangster rappers only dreamed about. Everything was white. The carpets were white, the tiles were white, the ceilings and walls were white, the sofas…well, they were champagne, because too much white can be counterproductive.

Out by the pool – and what a gigantic, full-of-clean-water, turdless, deep pool it was, too – guests stood around, sipping champagne from tall glasses, mumbling at one another in that way they always do in such scenes: *Rhubarb, rhubarb, rhubarb*, and so on and so forth. Occasionally, someone would say something hilarious, eliciting a haughty laugh from whomever heard it, but those incidents were few and far between, and thusly not worthy of mention.

A tinkle upon the side of a glass suggested someone wanted to make a speech, and so all those people going, "Rhubarb, rhubarb, rhubarb," stopped what they were doing for a moment and turned to face the glass-tinkler. One man mustn't have got the message, and so continued to say "Rhubarb" until someone donked him on the head with a cricket-bat and carried him outside, to where there should have been a waiting ambulance but wasn't, as it was still parked outside the new RadioShack in the high-street.

"Ladies and Gentlemen," said the tinkler of the glass, none other than Harry Hunter himself. He looked good for his age, as most people married to former porn-stars do. That wasn't to say he hadn't heard of Viagra; he just didn't need as much of it to wake the wee beastie as most geriatric gents. "I want to thank you all for making this party a huge success."

Cheers went up around the mansion, and the

people partaking in an orgy in the master bedroom stopped what they were doing for a moment, had a little breather, and patted one another on the bare backs, before continuing.

"I see a lot of familiar faces here today," said Hunter. "I've had the pleasure of working with many of you, and some of you have even had a go on Ivana, though not since we married, I'm pleased to say."

The crowd laughed heartily. A handsome, well-groomed man slipped sheepishly out the back door.

"Ah, Miss Treat!" Hunter said, spotting the supermodel in the middle of the room, nursing a large cocktail. "You look…healthy." And by 'healthy' he meant 'orange a fuck'. "And how nice it was of you to bring a handicapped person to such a lavish affair. You're such a darling."

Martha Blankenship didn't know where to look as all eyes fell upon her, so she settled upon the floor. Handicapped, indeed!

"Where's Ivana? Ivana?" Harry glanced about the place, searching for his delightful wife, as did everyone else. Eventually, she appeared from one of the adjacent rooms, slightly breathless and with her thong in her pocket (not that pocket). "Ah, beautiful wife of mine," said Hunter over the raucous applause. "Doesn't she look beautiful today, people?"

"As beautiful as anyone who's had ten mile of cock can look," muttered someone in the crowd, but fortunately it went mostly unheard. Those in the near vicinity of said line stifled sniggers. It was all in good jest, but then it always was when it wasn't your own wife on the receiving end. And Ivana Hunter had been on many a receiving end.

Harry Hunter pulled his wife in beneath his arm and waited until the crowd died down once again before speaking. "Many of you are still in the industry. Some of you have retired from it, slightly diseased but with a decent pension, and, well, some of you are here for the free food and, dare I say, finger buffet taking place right now in the master bedroom." This got a few laughs, but then it would, wouldn't it? "But I want you all to know that Ivana and I consider each and every one of you friends."

"With benefits," said Ivana, licking her lips seductively. A woman emerged from the adjacent room – the one Ivana had emerged from only a moment ago – and let herself out the back door. Some people think bisexuals are just greedy, but

LARRY II: THE SQUEEQUEL

they're just jealous only one side of the stamp is sticky for themselves.

"This party is going to be happening all day and all night, so make sure you pace yourselves." Hunter motioned to the punch-pond to his right. People were gathered around it, wielding ladles and pint glasses. "Or get shit-faced and have a good time, whatever floats your boat. I'm pleased to announce that the pool is now open for those of you that brought your costumes," — a huge cheer erupted in the hall — "and if you haven't brought a costume, don't let that stop you. We have an excellent pool-cleaner, Jiminéz. He specialises in pubic hairs and—"

"Darling," said Ivana. "Let's not embarrass Jimi." At the side of the room, a man holding a net and a pair of waders blushed. The crowd erupted with laughter once again, proving that they would laugh at pretty much anything, providing there was free booze at the end of it.

"Sorry about that," said Hunter. "Sorry Jiminéz," he added, drawing attention to the man at the edge of the room. "Ladies and gentlemen, that's Jiminéz right there. If anyone has an accident in the pool, he'll be there, net ready—"

"Harry," whispered Ivana.

"Yes, indeed, righty-ho! Everyone, please enjoy yourselves, and if you need anything, I'll be knocking about the place. Mi casa es su casa, and whatnot." And with that, the crowd went wild. Hunter and Ivana moved through the sea of people, Hunter leading the way, and arrived at Sam Treat, supermodel extraordinaire, and her apparently handicapped assistant.

"So pleased you could make it, Sam," Hunter said, leaning in and kissing the supermodel upon at least three of her cheeks. Ivana hissed like an angry cat, but that was just the way she was. "And you are?"

"I'm Martha," said Martha.

Hunter looked taken aback. "Oh!" said he. "It can talk, how wonderful!"

Martha knocked back her champagne and took herself off to the toilet, where she would cry for a few moments before taking a massive dump in the golden cistern.

"It's been too long," said Hunter. "The last time I saw you, you were down here." He held his hand about waist height. Ivana hissed again. "I meant she was but a child," said the former lothario to his wife (not to be confused with the bishop to the clown, nor the hooker to the priest).

LARRY II: THE SQUEEQUEL

"How is life in your neck of the woods, Sam?"

"It's been something of a nightmare recently," said Sam, grabbing a full glass from a passing waiter's tray. "Lost a couple of contracts; Maybelline, Estee Lauder, Scalextric."

"I hear Willy Wonka's hiring," slurred Ivana.

"Now, dear," Hunter said. "Play nice." To Sam he said, "My apologies, Sam. I haven't changed her litter tray for a few days, and she's starting to get a bit testy. Now where were we?"

Sam didn't want to dwell on her recent failings, and so changed the subject pretty smartish. "Loving the mansion," she said. "Everything's so…white."

"Ah," said Hunter. "That was Ivana's idea. The stains don't show up as much on white, but those champagne sofas can be a nightmare to scrub. I told her, I said let's get white sofas, but too much white can be counterproductive, apparently."

"So they say," said Sam. "You'll have to excuse the current hue. Bit of a mix-up at the tanning salon. Heads will roll."

"I'm sure they already have," said Hunter, turning to an invisible camera and tapping knowingly at his nose.

"What was that?" asked Sam. "You playing up

to the 3D? I don't think we're quite there yet."

"It was…just…I was…never mind," said Hunter. "So, are you here for the duration?"

"I was going to stick around for a few days," Sam said, "but that might not be the case anymore, not while there's a masked maniac on the loose. We all know what happens to the bimbos in such situations."

"We do indeed," said Ivana, surreptitiously grabbing a handful of crotch belonging to a passing waiter. He made a strange noise in his throat, handed Ivana a drink, and limped away, off to the kitchen to…readjust himself.

"Terrible things happening out there in the real world," said Hunter, motioning to the huge window to their right. "I remember the days you could leave your front door unlocked. Try doing that in this day and age. You'd be de-pantsed and buggered by a member of ISIS within the hour. And then while you're lying there, sobbing into your Horlicks, along comes a drone to finish the job the sodomising terrorist started. It really is a terrible state of affairs."

"I'm not sure it's all that bad, dear," said Ivana.

"Really? Try telling that to the poor old dear who only popped into town for a pack of beef jerky a few years ago." Hunter shook his head and clicked his tongue. "Horrible, horrible day that was, especially for the men involved."

"Did I miss anything?" said Martha, returning from the bathroom with her slap reapplied and just the right amount of toilet paper protruding from her skirt.

Ivana Hunter vomited into her glass. Harry Hunter apologised profusely ("She's never been very good with animals,") before dragging his wife away to get her cleaned up.

"Great party," Martha said as she danced The Running Man, followed quickly by The Panting Man. "Whew. Fancy a swim?"

23
An Alleyway (We've Been Here Once Before, Remember?)

Eric Roberts was halfway through arranging his DVD collection (*Best of the Best, Best of the Best 2* – it wasn't much of a collection, but why would it be? He had nothing to play them on) when a woman burst into the alleyway, screaming bloody murder. Actually, what she was screaming was, "Help! Help! There's a psycho in a pig mask and he's trying to kill me! Help! Help!" Eric Roberts almost fell out of his tree.

As the screaming woman passed beneath him – silly heels to be wearing if you're being pursued by a maniac – Eric leapt down, pulled his gi tight, and did three press-ups, for it was suicide going into battle without a half-decent warm-up. By the time he was back on his feet, the psycho was standing just a few metres away, regarding him warily. *And rightly so*, thought Eric Roberts. *I'm an ass-kicking maniac, liable to go full-on Gary Busey at any moment.*

"I know what you're thinking," Eric Roberts said to the porcine freak, who wasn't thinking anything, really, other than the woman who had just got away. "You're thinking I look a lot like Eric Roberts, aren't you?"

"Who?" said Pigface.

"Eric Roberts. You know? Famous movie star."

"I've heard of *Julia* Roberts," said Pigface. "Never heard of an *Eric* Roberts."

"Well you're hearing of one *now*, chump!" said Eric Roberts – *the* Eric Roberts, from the movies – as he moved into a fighting stance. "And you sure picked the wrong alleyway to chase screaming women through. Prepare to meet thy—"

"Thy?" said Pigface. "Are you a fucking musketeer or something?"

"If I was, would you be a little bit more scared of me?"

"A little."

"Then call me Porthos and prepare to have the shit kicked out of you." And with that, Eric Roberts unleashed a torrent of blows upon the man in the pig mask; some of them even connected.

Who does this guy think he is? said the mask as a flukey jab clobbered it just below the eyehole. *We don't have time for this nonsense.*

"I don't have time for this nonsense," said Eric

Roberts, breathless and sweaty and doubled over, gasping for air. "Return from whence you came and we'll call it quits."

Pigface sighed and pulled the axe from the belt of his trousers. "Squeeeeeee!" said he, bringing the axe around in a wide arc. Eric Roberts threw up an arm, and watched, helplessly, as it flew off into the distance.

"That was my hitting arm!" said Eric Roberts.

Go for his kicking leg! urged the mask, and Pigface did just that, swinging the axe low and true. As the leg fell away, the man in the Karate gi tottered back and forth, face ashen, boxers full.

"Okay, we'll call it a draw," said Eric Roberts, "but only because you caught me on an off day. Go on. Away with you, before I change my mind!"

"Squeeeeeeeeee!" squeeed Pigface. So bored had he become of decapitating people that he dropped the axe and lunged for the man in the gi, knocking him backwards. He landed on top of the half-person, growling and snarling, and pushed his thumbs into the man's eye-sockets. There was an audible pop! and then blood began to seep from the hollows.

"My seeing eyes!" screamed Eric Roberts. "You absolute bastard!"

LARRY II: THE SQUEEQUEL

Put him out of his misery, mumbled the mask. *It's something his agent should have done years ago.*

"Run away now, before it's too late!" said the blind, one-armed, one-legged former movie-star. "I'm warning you, this won't end well for you!"

Pigface had had enough. It was bad enough that he'd lost a kill because of this prick; the silly fucker didn't know when he'd been bested. Best of the Bested?

That's a terrible joke, said the mask. *Don't let it happen again.*

Latching on to either side of the man's head, Pigface twisted as hard as he could. There was an almighty crack, and then Eric Roberts fell very still – apart from the occasional twitch, which was to only be expected.

Three thousand miles away, on the set of her latest masterpiece, Julia Roberts' suddenly threw her arms back and dropped to her knees. An ethereal light swirled around her, fizzing magically. "There can be only one!" she cried.

Hard to believe, but true.

24
A Bus

"What's wrong with that girl's eyes?" asked a rotund lady sitting on the seats (I *said* she was rotund) opposite. "Where have her pupils fucked off to?"

Sister Geoff, who had taken up position in the middle of the aisle, said, "She's currently in a trance which gives her access to the mind and vision of a geriatric pig-faced slasher from Camp Diamond Creek."

"Oh," said the talking circle. "She should see a doctor about that."

"It's too late to start a new running joke now," said the nun. "If you're interested, we've got one about watches. You could always give that a shot."

The rotund woman glanced down at her watch, for she always liked to get involved in running jokes. Plus, you had a much better chance of appearing in the final book if you were seen to be interacting with the main lot. It was a pity, then, that she hadn't seen her watch since 1991. It was there – beneath the layers of arm fat – but it was about as easy to get to as the International Space Station. It was also the reason her left hand was

LARRY II: THE SQUEEQUEL

constantly blue.

Forgetting the watch, she turned her attention back to her book: *How to Engage Strangers on a Bus for Idiots.*

"This one's gone on for a bit," said Mayor Ketchum. He was sitting to Amanda's right, in a piece of chewing-gum, in fact, but that's not important right now. "Should we give her a gentle slap, or something?"

"I dare you," said Freddy, who was sitting to Amanda's left, holding her back by the shoulder so that she didn't topple forward and face-plant the bus floor. The mayor had already pulled back an open hand when Freddy added, "It was a *joke*, Mayor. Never wake a sleeping baby. Let sleeping dogs lie. Never slap a trancing woman, and all that." The mayor retracted his hand, and not a moment too soon as Amanda's eyes rolled down into the correct position, and she regarded him suspiciously.

"Were you going to slap me?" she said.

"Of course not," said the mayor.

"Yes you were," said Sister Geoff. "You said 'This one's gone on for a bit. Should we give her a—"

"Few more minutes to come round,"

interrupted the mayor, shooting evils at the nun. Turning back to Amanda, he said, "What did you see?"

Amanda frowned. "It was really bizarre," she said. "I saw Julia Roberts in a gi, but she looked…ill."

"That's not Julia Roberts," said the mayor. "That's her brother, Eric."

"Never heard of him," said Sister Geoff.

"He's a bit of a hobo," the mayor went on. "We let him sleep in a tree in an alleyway. He keeps himself to himself."

"What happened to him?" asked Freddy.

"Well, after The Dark Knight, he went full-on Gary Busey—"

"No," said Freddy. "I meant what happened to him in Amanda's vision."

"Pigface lopped an arm and leg off and gouged his eyes out," said Amanda.

"Shit!" said the mayor, and a very apt use of the word it was, too. "That means he's almost at the Hunter mansion. It's only a few streets away from Roberts' alleyway."

"Can this thing go any faster?" Sister Geoff bellowed at the driver.

The driver put his foot down, thusly managing

LARRY II: THE SQUEEQUEL

to get 40kph out of the bus.

"Not really worth it, was it?" said the nun. "Good job Keanu Reeves isn't on this bus. We'd be fucking incinerated by now." A child, no older than four, tugged on Sister Geoff's tunic, revealing the shotgun she had secreted there. "Bang!" said the nun, and the child, rushing back to its mother – who was too busy talking on her phone to notice – began to cry.

"God help us all," said the mayor.

And the bus trickled onward.

25
The Hunter Mansion

Well, this looks like it could be fun, said the mask.

Larry stood at the end of the driveway, staring up at the house and the people mingling just outside its huge doors, smoking, chatting, and drinking from crystal flutes. "Perfect place for a final showdown," said Larry. He'd just had a strange vision in which a nun had reduced a child to tears. "This is where we'll find our final girl."

Well, we can't just rock up at the party looking like this, said the mask, and rightly so.

"Oh, I'm sorry," said Larry. "I forgot to pack my tuxedo on account that I don't fucking own one."

Alright, Porky, we'll just have to improvise.

"If, by improvise, you mean kill everyone in sight, then I can give it a bloody good go." He reached for his axe.

"Excuse me?"

Larry did an about turn, and then did a squeal. Standing there, in glamorous tuxedos and dresses (not at the same time, of course) were a group of people wearing pig masks. It would have been ridiculous, under any other circumstances…no, it was ridiculous. Just plain ridiculous under *these* circumstances.

"You must have missed the memo," said the one at the front. The one at the front is normally the leader, and that certainly appeared to be the case here. "We agreed to meet at The Swan with Two Dicks instead of outside the gates."

Larry shrugged, for he was completely bereft of words. Unfortunately, his mask wasn't. *What the fuck is going on here?* it said. *This must be some kind of nightmare. Did you fall asleep again, you daft cu—*

"I hope we're not late for the pig orgy," muffled a woman's voice. "Paul, we're not going to be late for the pi—"

"No, *Cynthia*, we're not late," said the leader – Paul, apparently. He glanced down at his watch. It was a cross-dresser's watch, inasmuch as it wasn't exactly sure what the time was, but whatever the time was, it just felt right. "Honestly, it's like she's never been to a pig orgy before."

Larry snorted. "Amateurs," said he, for it seemed the right kind of thing to say.

This is perfect, said the mask. *Play along. These buffoons are our ticket inside.*

"Do you have your ticket to get inside?" asked Paul.

Fuck, said the mask.

Larry patted himself down. "Shit!" he said. "It must have fallen out of my pocket on the way here."

"You don't have any pockets," said Paul.

"That's why I don't have a ticket then," said Larry.

Just then, the one called Cynthia stepped forward, and in her hand were two tickets. "You might as well have Sid's," she said, handing Larry one of the tickets. "He chickened out at the last minute."

Well, thank you, Sid, said the mask.

"Thank you Cynthia," said Larry. He glanced down at the ticket, which was printed on special paper, as most orgy invites are (not that I'd know). "Squeal like a piggy at Harry Hunter's Pig Orgy!" Larry said, reading the ticket verbatim.

"It's a *Deliverance* reference," said Paul. "You know, with the banjos and the toothless rednecks?"

"I once knew a man who broke his banjo during a particularly frantic wank," said Cynthia.

The male members of the pig-masked group suddenly crossed their legs and hissed through their teeth. "Thanks for sharing that," said Paul.

LARRY II: THE SQUEEQUEL

"Shall we go inside?"

"Sounds good to me."

"Squeeee!"

"How can you break your banjo?"

And along the never-ending driveway they went, just a band of horny piggies. Nothing to see here, move along. Those standing outside the mansion, just milling around or smoking, watched as the drove of pigs – the collective noun for horny pigs is a *fuckit*, but in this instance, at least one of the pigs wasn't horny, just eager to start killing people – made their way toward the manse. One woman, who looked like she had been dragged through a hedge backwards, was doubled over, vomiting over a clematis.

"Aye, aye," said Paul, who definitely was the leader in this case – and also the one most likely to rabbit punch (piggy pummel?) a fellow orgy-member during coitus. "Looks like Hunter's spared no expense with security. He motioned toward the two huge men standing between the huge door-frame staring down at a huge clipboard. These were your stereotypical doormen. Black bomber-jackets, Doc Martens, skin-heads, tattoos on their faces.

I don't like the look of them, said the mask.

"They don't like the look of us," said Larry.

"Play it cool, son," said Paul from the corner of his mouth. "We've got our passes, and we've adhered to the dress-code."

"*I* haven't," Larry said. "I'm wearing a white apron with blood down it."

"Each to their own," said Paul. "Look, we'll talk them round. Everyone has their price, especially doormen."

As they got within spitting distance of the doormen – Larry knew it was spitting distance because something warm and sticky landed on his right hand – the doormen began to mutter to one another. Never a good sign when one wants to gain entrance to somewhere. Even though he had an axe down his trousers, Larry felt more than a little unnerved by these bald gorillas.

"And what do we have here?" said the gorilla on the right. We'll call him Dum, though not to his face, of course.

"Looks like someone left the sty gate open," said the other one, Dee, as he gave each of the pigs a once-over. "I've seen some shit in my time, but nothing as freaky as this, and I was an altar-boy."

"Are we late for the pig orgy?" asked Paul, quite confidently, Larry thought, for a man talking to a

LARRY II: THE SQUEEQUEL

pair of belt-buckles. He held his ticket out and Dum took it, read it (or at least looked at the picture) and handed it back.

"It ain't started yet, has it Dee?" said Dum.

"Not that I know of," said Dum. "There's a regular orgy on up there at the moment, and they'll probably have to give everything a good wipe down once they're finished, so I'd imagine you've got time to grab yourself a trough of something nice and sparkly."

"Ha, I see what you did there," said Paul. "Trough…very clever…so, if you two strapping gents would like to step aside, we'll be out of your hai…out of your eyebrows in no time."

"Not a problem," said Dum, stepping down off the steps and creating a man-shaped aperture for the drove to make their way through.

"Thanks very much," said Paul, and he was about to lead the way when—

"Ow!" said Larry. "Take your hairy paws off me!"

Don't insult the giant, said the mask. *Especially when he has his hairy paws on us.*

"This one ain't adhered to the proper dress-code," said Dum, squeezing Larry's shoulder harder.

"No, that one definitely can't come in," said Dee.

There was a moment of awkward silence, as is to be expected when you're trying to build an atmosphere, and then Paul said, "Oh, okay. He's not with us anyway," before continuing on into the mansion, followed by the majority of his group.

"Whatever happened to honour amongst piggies?" said Cynthia, the only one who remained behind. "Look, boys, what's it going to take for you to allow my porcine friend here to pass?"

Watch it, Larry, said the mask. *I think this one's got a bit of a soft spot for you.*

Judging by the size of her backside, Larry guessed she had a *lot* of a soft spot, and for anyone brave enough to approach it.

The doormen exchanged a glance. You could hear hamster wheels turning, but only if you listened very carefully. "What do you think, Dee?" said Dum.

"I reckon twenty dollars and a blowy around the back ought to cover it," said Dee.

"How about thirty dollars and we skip the blowy?" said Cynthia, already rifling through her purse.

"What about thirty-five, and you just appraise

LARRY II: THE SQUEEQUEL

our manhoods?" said Dum, hopeful.

"How's about forty, and I just tell you that they look both look well?" Cynthia held out a pair of notes.

"Deal," said Dum, snatching the notes and handing one to his partner-in-slime. "And phew. I've got this lump that's really been bothering me, but if you say it's nothing, then that's good enough for me."

"Step aside, boys," said Cynthia, and she hooked her arm into the crook of Larry's. "We've got some pigs to fuck."

26
An Alleyway (It's on **Google Maps**, if you don't believe me)

"Jesus Christ!" said Sister Geoff, crossing her heart repeatedly. "Looks like someone shaved Julia Roberts and then gouged her eyes out with a pair of fat thumbs."

And that was exactly what it looked like. Lying there in the middle of the alleyway, already swamped by opportunistic flies, was Eric Roberts; former movie-star and uncanny lookalike to a current movie starlet.

"I've never seen anything so horrible in all my life," said Mayor Ketchum. "And I was—"

"Let me guess," said Freddy. "An altar-boy?"

"I was going to say 'son of a preacher-man'," said the mayor, "but close enough."

Sister Geoff prodded the mangled corpse with her foot. "We can't just leave him out here like this," she said. "He's not Gary Busey, you know."

"We don't have time to muck about," said Amanda. "Mayor, can you alert the cops, get them to head over to Harry Hunter's? Tell them we've got a dead nobody in an alleyway that needs picking up, and a star on Hollywood's Walk of

LARRY II: THE SQUEEQUEL

Fame which needs to be scratched off?"

"Oh, I'm sorry," said the mayor. "I appear to have left my fucking Bat Signal at home."

"Some mayor," muttered Sister Geoff.

"Arguing ain't going to get us anywhere," said Freddy. He'd gathered a handful of throwing stars which he'd found scattered around the body. He'd never thrown a throwing star before, but how hard could it be?

"Ow, you little prick," said Sister Geoff as she yanked the throwing star out of her thigh.

Freddy apologised profusely and tucked the remainder of the stars away in his pocket for later.

"Come on," said Amanda. "Let's just hope we're not too late."

"We're always too late," said Sister Geoff.

Which was true.

27
The Hunter Mansion

Sam Treat had spent the last fifteen minutes searching the mansion for Martha, only to find the poor moose upchucking on a clematis out front. The *fuckit* of pigs she passed on the way outside was a little unsettling, and in pretty poor taste, given the recent murders.

"Are you okay?" Sam said, peeling her assistant's sick-matted hair away from her face.

"Never better," said Martha. "Remind me to steer clear of the hors d'oeuvres. I think they've been spiked."

Back in the mansion (it only cost twenty dollars and a blowy out back), Sam cleaned Martha up in the toilets and led her back out into the crowd. "This isn't the best party we've ever been to," she said. "I think I was expecting more of Harry Hunter." She had heard all about how Hunter parties were legendary, usually from the point of view of people who'd never been to one. Honestly, she didn't see what all the fuss was about.

"Worth flying three-thousand-miles for?" said Martha, the colour returning to her cheeks.

Sam plucked a flute of champagne from a

passing waiter's tray and downed it in one. The waiter muttered something under his breath – "Thirsty bitch," it was, not that anyone had heard it – before disappearing into the throng. "In all honesty, I don't think I've ever been so utterly bored in my entire life," said Sam.

"One more drink and then back to the hotel?" said Martha, optimistically.

"Sounds good to me," said her beautiful boss as she wiped a hand across her face. "Look at this," she said, holding said hand out. It was awfully orange. It was so orange that the satsumas sitting in a nearby fruit-bowl got jealous. Sam hadn't seen anything that orange since David Hasselhoff whipped his dick out at a gig in Germany. It was so orange—

"Can we stop with the orange jokes?" said Martha.

"Sorry, I must have been thinking out loud," replied Sam. "Okay, one more drink and then we're offski. Now, where did that waiter get off to?"

'That waiter' was getting off to Ivana Hunter's naked body in the snooker room, and wouldn't be finished for quite some time.

*

"This is exciting, isn't it?" said Cynthia. "We'll be

getting off soon."

"Already?" said Larry. "But we've only just arrived."

"No…I meant…never mind."

They were standing at the edge of the room, of which there were four. Ten little piggies, all in a row. There was a nursery rhyme in there somewhere, but for the life of him, Larry couldn't remember it. Something about roast beef and wee-wees…

At the centre of the room stood a hog. A huge, hulking, derobed hog with tusks that looked liable to do some real damage, or cause some real pleasure, depending on which way you looked at it.

Larry looked at it as an obstacle, for when the time came – and it would be very soon, according to his little charred non-penis – the hog would be the first to go.

"Boars and Sows, and if we're really lucky, gilts," said the hog.

"What's a gilt?" asked Larry.

"Virgin pig," said Cynthia.

"Are *you* a gilt?" asked Larry.

"Not since I was fourteen," said Cynthia. "I've had more miles of cock than—"

"Can we all pay attention to the hog, please?"

said the hog, irritably. Cynthia shut up, for she wanted to be on the right side of those tusks when the time came ("or when she came," said the parson to the failed actress.) "Thank you. Now, before we start rutting, I want to lay a few ground rules. Some of them are common sense. For example, no chokeholds. We do have a stretcher, and I believe Paul is trained in the art of CPR, but I'd rather not find out just how good he is."

This was met by snorts and nods of approval. Larry didn't bother.

"If a sow is not interested in you, do not force yourself upon her. We're pigs, not Italians. I'm running a three strikes and you're out policy this afternoon, unless, of course, you're striking someone for pleasure, in which case, avoid the face. A gentle slap on the ass is worth two in the bush, so to speak."

A sow at the edge of the room raised her hand. "Yes?"

"Can we defecate?"

The hog sighed. "I'd rather we didn't. If you haven't noticed, everything in this room is white. Everything in the mansion is white, except for those weird champagne sofas. I'm sure the last thing Harry Hunter wants to discover, once we've packed up and gone home, is a room full of pig-shit.

The sow nodded solemnly.

"We have…" He looked down at his watch. It was the kind of watch a sexually-confused hog might wear; one of those hulking black things from the 1980s, you know? The ones with a calculator? "Two hours from when I say 'Soueee'."

Good job he went for 'Soueee', said the mask. *We've got the trademark on Squeee.*

"And finally," said the hog, "have *fun*. That's what we're here for, after all. Let's get this party started."

Nobody moved a muscle.

"I mean *'Soueee'!"*

Everyone rushed for the centre of the room.

Everyone except for Larry, whose limited knowledge of sex and the doing thereof – not to mention the fact his winkle resembled a scorched whelk – would keep him side-lined for the duration.

*

"Wow!" said Freddy, staring up at Hunter's mansion. "This place is off the hook."

"Never speak like that again," said Amanda.

"Fo shizzle," said Freddy.

LARRY II: THE SQUEEQUEL

The gravel crunched beneath their feet as they approached the manse; four of the most diverse protagonists imaginable, riding into the final battle on invisible horses. As analogies went, it wasn't much of one, but you get what you pay for.

"Halt!" said one of the giants (Dee) standing outside the mansion's front door. He was smoking a tailor-made, which was barely visible in his gorilla-sized fist, but the smoke was a dead giveaway.

"Yes! Halt!" said the second giant, Dum, who was smoking a pipe, perhaps to make it easier for the newcomers to differentiate between the two of them. "We'll have no trouble here today, so go on your merry way and we'll speak no more about this chance encounter."

"What the eff are you babbling on about?" said Sister Geoff.

"Ah!" said Dee. "A talking penguin! En-garde!" And with that, he dropped down into a perfect fencer's stance, if you were happy for your fence to come without trellis.

"Dee?" said Dum. "That is a nun, if I'm not mistaken."

"Don't be silly, man!" said the one ready for battle. "Nuns don't exist in real life. This isn't fucking Mordor!"

"And talking penguins are ten a penny in Haddon, are they?" said Mayor Ketchum, who had had quite enough of this silliness.

"You," said Dee, straightening up and taking a pull on his roll-yer-own. "You're the mayor."

"I am indeed," said the mayor.

"Don't you have any shops you should be opening?" said Dum, snipping at the air with his fingers, of which he only had three, and one of them was a thumb.

"Yes, yes, very funny, ha ha," said the mayor. "Look, lads, spot of bother. We have reason to believe that there is a killer in there, and he's about to go full-on Gary Busey on the guests."

The giants exchanged a dubious glance. Then, they erupted with laughter. Well of course they did. Whoever heard of such nonsense? A killer, indeed.

"We're telling the truth!" Amanda said, taking a few steps forward. "He's a real psycho and he'll stop at nothing to quench his thirst for blood and gore."

The doormen laughed some more.

"Stop!" said Dum, doubled over and red as an apple (not a green apple, though). "You're killing me!"

"'He'll stop at nothing'," mocked Dee. "For shits and giggles, what does this psycho look like?"

"He wears a pig mask," said Freddy. "And a white apron, and he likes to say 'Squeee' a lot, probably because he has a trademark on it, or something."

The doormen ceased with their uncontrollable laughter, proving that it wasn't uncontrollable after all. "A pig mask, you say?" said Dum.

"Yeah," said Amanda. "You haven't let anyone in wearing a pig mask, have you?"

"Of course they haven't," said Sister Geoff. "That would be ridiculous, wouldn't it boys?"

The boys nodded in unison, though neither were forthcoming with speech, at least not for thirty seconds or so, by which time Sister Geoff had shimmied halfway up a drainpipe in an attempt to gain entry. One slip later, and she was lying at the giants' feet, winded, and with a shotgun halfway up her—

"Hunter's allowing people in as pigs today," said Dee, scratching his bald phizzog. "There's an orgy—"

"A *pig* orgy," interrupted Dum. "We just let a…what's the collective noun for horny pigs?"

"A *fuckit*," said Freddy.

"We just let a fuckit of pigs into the mansion, and they were all wearing pig masks." Dum pushed his broken nose up so that it resembled a snout.

Amanda couldn't believe what she was hearing. "How convenient that this pig orgy falls on the same day a maniac in a pig mask comes to town," said she.

"Synchronicity works in mysterious ways," said Freddy.

"That's *God*," said Sister Geoff. "And this isn't synchronicity at work. This is a crazy plot device to get to the end of the…I want to say film, but it feels more like a book."

"You *have* to let us in," Amanda said to the towering doormen.

"No we don't," said Dee. "That's why we're doormen. We get to pick and choose who gets past us. Sometimes we let a fucking idiot in, but part of the job is knowing that if that happens, we can always throw them back out again later on. Usually by the scruff of their neck, like they used to do in olden days London."

"He's in there, and *you* allowed that to happen," said the mayor. "Now step aside, before I break out the harsh language and pointy finger."

LARRY II: THE SQUEEQUEL

"You can go in," said Dum, "but we'll have to charge you, the same as we've charged everyone else."

"How much?" said Amanda, checking her purse for change.

"Twenty each and a blowy from the nun," said Dum. He made a sex face at Sister Geoff. Sister Geoff kicked him in the bollocks.

"That was a bit uncalled for," said Dee, helping his moaning brethren up from the gravel. "Aren't nuns supposed to be nice. Gentle and kind?"

"You're thinking of fairies," said Sister Geoff. "And I eat fairies for breakfast, so unless you want a hoof to the gonads like your friend here, keep your hands to yourself and step the fuck back."

Dee did as he was told, and in the process cleared a path to the door.

"Come on," said the nun, leading the way into the mansion. "I'm drier than a nun's tasty, if you get my meaning."

"Gandhi's flip-flop would have worked better," said the mayor, following the nun closely.

Out of the frying pan, into the fire, Amanda thought as she crossed the threshold.

*

"Is that a nun getting pissed?" said Sam Treat,

motioning to the punch bowl. As a supermodel, she thought she'd seen everything, and now, she could safely say that she had.

The nun, for it definitely wasn't a talking penguin, had eschewed the ladles completely and had gone for the kill, face-planting the punchbowl as if it was nothing more than an oasis, liable to disappear at any given moment.

"Must be having a bad day," said Martha. "Mind you, if I was a nun, I'd get pissed at every opportunity, too."

"Looks like she's being reprimanded by Hunter now."

Harry Hunter had dragged the nun out of the punchbowl by her legs and was giving her a thorough dressing down. The nun's response was to kick the ageing lothario in the shin, and as the host hopped about screaming blood murder – actually he was screaming, "Fucking nuns! Bastards think they own the world!" but that was neither here nor there – the nun was ushered away by a young couple and a man who looked like he should be mayor.

"This party keeps getting weirder and weirder," said Sam.

"Doesn't it just?" said Martha.

LARRY II: THE SQUEEQUEL

*

Larry didn't know where to look, for there were naked pigs as far as the eye could see, all commingling to create some sort of giant sexy swine monster. They were far too busy rutting to notice the impossibly sharp axe he now wielded.

"Squeeee-cough-cough-eeeee!" said he, lunging toward the beast with nine backs.

*

"Just having a bit of fun," said the nun, peeling a slice of orange away from her forehead. "You fuckers need to lighten up."

"We're here for Pigface," said Amanda. "Remember? And we need you sober. Latin's a bugger of a language at the best of times."

"I don't do Latin," said Sister Geoff.

"What?"

"It's a dead language. What's the fucking point in learning a dead language?"

"But you're a nun," said Freddy. "All nuns speak Latin."

"This one doesn't," said Sister Geoff. "Spanish, a little bit of Klingon, and English, of course, but that's all you're getting from me."

"Fucking marvellous," said the mayor. "How are we going to vanquish the demon now? I'm pretty sure yelling at it in Klingon isn't going to do the trick."

Just then, an ear-splitting *Squeee*™ echoed around the mansion.

A second later, a severed pig's head landed in the punchbowl.

*

Go for the one with the little dick! screamed the mask. *Take his fucking face off!*

Larry swung the axe down and watched as it *thunked* into he of the tiny phallus. "How dare you pretend to be pigs!" he bellowed. "Pigs are noble creatures. You lot are a disgrace!" He yanked the axe free and turned on the next naked pig – a sow he recognised.

"Why are you doing this?" Cynthia screeched, pressing herself up against the wall.

Larry's answer was short and to the point. "Squeee!" he said

Of course he did.

He swung the axe once again.

*

"Everybody calm down," said Harry Hunter, who had taken to a makeshift podium – a white chair, in fact – in the middle of the room. "This is all part of the show."

LARRY II: THE SQUEEQUEL

"No it's bloody not!" someone from the frantic crowd shouted.

"If you could all calmly make your way out onto the driveway – and what a splendid driveway it is, if I do say so myself – that would be fantastic."

But there was no calming down this crowd, who hadn't anticipated a massacre when they'd climbed out of bed that very morn, and were a little bit pissed off they were in the middle of one right now. But that's the thing with massacres. You don't see them coming until it's too late, by which time you've got an arm off and you've shit your knickers…

"Has anyone seen Ivana?" Hunter said, scouring the room for his wife. And then he too to shouting.

"Ivana!"

"Ivana!"

"Bloody hell, where is she?"

*

Ivana was, of course, in the arms of a waiter, whose name was something like Marco or Frederico or the like, not that it mattered as this Italian stallion hadn't even been given a line thus far and would therefore be dead by the end of this section.

"Did you hear something?" said Ivana, climbing sluggishly out of bed.

"I dida nota heara anythinga," said the Italian.

"Knock it off with the accent," said Ivana. "We both know you're from Boston."

Marco pulled his trousers on. "What did it sound like?" said he.

"It sounded like someone said *squeee*," said Ivana, peering through the crack in the door.

"Be careful with that," said Marco. "It might be trademarked. You don't want to end up in a one-bed apartment eating beans from a can." He walked across the room, picked up his tray – vol-au-vents, if you must know – and was about to leave the room when the door exploded inward. Ivana Hunter flew backwards where she clobbered into a wardrobe, but she didn't rest on her laurels (she didn't even know what laurels were) and quickly clambered back to her feet.

"Who the fuck are you?" gasped Marco, addressing the pig-masked maniac standing in the doorway. That axe of his looked ever so shiny, beneath all the blood and gore. Sharp, too.

"They call me Pigface," said Pigface. "And I'm about to—"

LARRY II: THE SQUEEQUEL

"Who does?" interrupted Marco.

Pigface slumped about the shoulders. "Excuse me?"

"*Who* calls you Pigface?"

"Them," said Pigface. "The…the people who *know* about me."

"I don't know about you," said Marco. "What should *I* call you?"

"Oh come on!" said Pigface. "You can call me Pigface as well. Actually, scratch that. It doesn't matter what you call me because you're going to be feeling the sharp end of *this* in a second." He raised his axe. A hunk of someone's face slipped from the blade and slapped the carpet beneath.

"Look at the *mess* you're making!" screeched Ivana. "Can't you see that everything's white!? Blood's an absolute nightmare to get out of—" She stopped speaking, as one is apt to do when one has an axe sticking out of one's face.

"Squeeeeee!" squealed Pigface.

"Bleurggggghhhhhhh," went Marco, bringing up vol-au-vents by the bucketload.

Pigface stalked across the room, pulled his axe out of the woman's face – thusly unpinning her from the wardrobe to which she was presently attached – and turned on the Italian stallion, who was ralphing his guts up next to the bed. By the time he realised he should have been making good his escape, it was too late.

Pigface was all over him like a mullet on a redneck. "Owa, thata hurtsa!" screamed Marco as Larry set about him with the axe.

"Shut up and take it like a man," said Pigface. "And everyone knows you're from Boston."

*

"We have to get out of here," said Sam Treat as she tried to battle her way through the screaming throng. "It's that maniac, the one that killed all those people. And now he's going to kill everyone in here because it's a sequel and the body-count has to be higher."

Martha Blankenship had taken to punching people in the head; even the ones who weren't doing the pushing. "Try to remain calm!" she grunted, open-hand-slapping a passing old lady. "We'll be out of here soon enough, if everyone would act rationally and calmly!" She head-butted an old man, who was about to complain about Martha's treatment of his fallen wife.

"I'm going to die in here!" screeched Sam. "People like me don't survive situations like this. We're usually the first to go."

LARRY II: THE SQUEEQUEL

"Well you've done well getting this far then haven't you?" said Martha, elbow-dropping a child (who shouldn't have been at the party in the first place, but that's what you get when you employ bald gorillas to man the doors).

"I'm not ready to die!" gasped Sam. "I've got so much to give!"

The irony was that people were more likely to get whatever it was she had to give once she was dead and gone.

*

"First floor!" Amanda said, snatching a knife up from the kitchen counter. It had been used to slice lemons, and so would sting a bit should she manage to slice the bastard with it. Then again, he was semi-immortal (just like Bob Hope and Bruce Forsythe) and therefore probably didn't feel pain the way he once had.

They were halfway up the first flight of stairs when the mutilated body of an Italian man – he looked like a Marco or Frederico to Amanda – toppled over the bannister and landed in the middle of the hall below with a sickening crunch.

"Bet Hunter's regretting opting for white now," said Freddy.

"Look!" said the mayor, pointing up to the

landing. "Is that the murderous bastard?"

Standing there, glancing down at the mayhem unfolding below, was Pigface. Now, three things happened in quick succession: Firstly, Pigface's gaze was drawn to the movement upon the staircase to his right. Secondly, he recognised two of the four people standing there, and thirdly, a nun flipped him the bird.

"You!" said Pigface. "You bitch!"

"I think he's talking to you," said Freddy to Amanda. "Must have made quite an impression."

"Must have," said Amanda, slowly traversing the staircase, unable to take her eyes off the maniac awaiting her on the first floor. So this was it…this was what it had all been building up to. The final showdown. The last stand. The—

"Will you be quiet," Amanda said.

"Sorry," said Freddy. "I must have been thinking out loud."

"Well don't. There's a good chance that, as a finale, this'll be a bit of a let-down."

"Don't be so hard on yourself," said Freddy. "It's going to be *tres* exciting. How could it *not* be? We've got a nun and a mayor." There was a joke in there somewhere, but for the life of him he couldn't find it.

LARRY II: THE SQUEEQUEL

"He's got an axe and a grudge," said Amanda. "I think that makes us about even."

And up the never-ending staircase they went. So long was this staircase that by the time they reached the first floor, Pigface had sodded off to somewhere else.

*

"Remind me why we're in here again?" said Dee.

"Hunter wants this bastard caught," replied Dum, slipping into his knuckleduster. "And what Hunter wants, Hunter gets."

"He must have really wanted Chlamydia," said Dee. "Hang on a minute. Where's my knuckleduster?"

"Did you *have* one?"

"No, but up until ten seconds ago, neither did you."

"I found it in my pocket," said Dum. "I think the director or author of this little fiasco is trying to help us. Check your pockets. You might be pleasantly surprised."

Dee did some checking, and came out with a banana. "What the fuck is this?" said he.

"Looks like a banana," said Dum. "Surprise!"

"SQUEEEE!" said Pigface as he leapt out of a broom cupboard. If this was a film, the audience would have just thrown popcorn all over themselves and the nervous-looking guy three rows back would have excused himself to the toilet, but it isn't, so there's no need to dwell on it.

"Prepare to die," said Dum.

"Yeah," added Dee, and he threw the banana at the pig-faced lunatic. As it bounced off and landed harmlessly on the white hallway rug, he said, "I thought it might have been a grenade in disguise, or something."

Dum rushed the maniac and managed to get a few punches in before the tables turned, and my, how they turned! Pigface grabbed onto the burly man's arm and, with a quick flick of the wrist, snapped it to the side. There was an audible crack and then the big man began to sob uncontrollably.

"I've got him!" said Dee, and he picked the banana up, located the pin (you didn't think it was a normal banana, did you?) and pulled it out. He rolled it along the hallway, and even though bananas aren't known for their rolling prowess, this one went just far enough. "Fire in the hole!"

The explosion was immense. There was a blinding white light and then an awful lot of fire. Dee flew back through the air – in super-slow-mo, no less. Somewhere, someone made a Wilhelm

LARRY II: THE SQUEEQUEL

Scream. It was like something from an Arnold Schwarzenegger movie, one of the ones without the pregnant man or Danny DeVito. For a banana, that thing really packed a punch.

When the dust and viscera settled, Dee climbed to his foot (the other one had been blown off) and stared into the smoky hallway. "Dum?" said he. "Say something if you're alive.

From the smoke rolled a head, and it was a head Dee recognised well. "Oh, man!" he said, dropping to his knees. "Oh, I am so sorry, bud." He picked the head up and cradled it. "Fuck, we didn't even get a chance to see ACDC, like we said we would. We didn't skydive or go to one of those paint-your-own-teapot parties people keep raving on about. OOOOOW!" he said, for it was only then that he realised he was missing his left foot – the one made famous by Daniel Day Lewis.

From within the smoke, something clattered. Dee dropped his friend's detached head. "No," said he, cutting through the gloom with sore eyes. "It can't be."

But it was. It bloody was! The lunatic in the pig mask came staggering forwards. "Who throws a banana?" he said. "I mean, really?" He raised the axe, and was about to bring it down on Dee's bald pate when…

*

Freddy thumped into Pigface, sending him back into the smoke. From somewhere behind, Amanda screamed, but it was too late for Freddy to change his mind now. This had to end now. Enough people had died – though technically, not enough to warrant a third in the franchise. It was, Freddy thought, time to stand up and be counted. He had a shot at being the hero this time around. The Final *Boy*. Like Jamie Lee Curtis, only with one extra bollock.

"Squeeeee!" said Pigface, holding the irritating boy at arm's length.

"Change the record, Porky," said Freddy, kicking the porcine maniac about the kneecaps, to no real effect.

"Get the bastard!" said the nun. "Send him straight to Hell, do not pass go, do not collect seventy virgins."

"You brought a nun!" Larry howled. "What's she going to do? *Latin* me to death?"

"Actually, she doesn't *know* Latin," grunted Freddy, putting a few feet (and a couple of arms) between himself and the beast, "so the joke's on you. Ha!"

LARRY II: THE SQUEEQUEL

Amanda stepped forward so that she was level with Freddy. "You were dead," she said. "We killed you."

"Best thing that ever happened to me," said Pigface. "Obviously not at the time. It smarted like a sonofabitch. But like any good slasher, I'm back, and this time I'm bringing home the bacon."

"What a terrible joke," said the mayor, and he'd been to a Joan Rivers gig.

"I haven't got a lot to work with," said Pigace. "And anyway, who the fuck are you? This is between me and the final girl, who, by the way, is the reason for all this."

Amanda visibly slumped. "You lie," she said.

"Only about masturbating on the back of my pig," said Pigface. "And occasionally when I want to get out of doing the dishes, but apart from that, I'm as honest as the next man."

"Why are we even *conversing* with it?" said Sister Geoff, and with that she pulled out the shotgun she'd been itching to use for the last hundred pages or so. She cocked it and unloaded both barrels into Pigface's piggy face.

"*Squeee!*" said he, and it was a lot louder than usual on account that the hole in the front of his face was suddenly a lot bigger. But then, something remarkable happened. Something that shouldn't have been possible. The chewed-up flesh and shattered bone that made up the lunatic's exploded phizzog began to writhe and squirm. It was like something out of an early Peter Jackson movie, before he started piddling about with Hobbits.

"Shoot it again!" said Mayor Ketchum.

"Got no more shells!" shouted the nun, though quite why she shouted she wasn't sure. She took a tentative step forwards and slammed the butt of the shotgun into the thing's pulsating face. The head snapped back a little, but apart from that it was something of an anti-climax.

"Hit it again!" yelled the mayor.

"Didn't you just hear the narrator?" said the nun. "It's fucking pointless!"

"The snout's back!" yelled Freddy.

"Why are we all shouting!?" shouted Amanda. "Quick, pin it down!"

At first, those present weren't sure they had heard correctly, and so there were a lot of frowns and a lot of exchanged glances. Amanda, however, was already leading by example, and had latched onto Pigface's right arm and was dragging it down to the ground.

LARRY II: THE SQUEEQUEL

"If you say so," said Freddy, and grabbed Pigface's left arm. Between them, they manage to get the bastard onto his back, and still his face continued to reconstruct itself, and what an ugly face it was, too. A face only a mother could love, and even then only in small doses.

"Get his legs!" Amanda squealed. And the mayor, who had nothing better to do – not without a pair scissors and a ribbon, anyway – dropped to his knees and sat on Pigface's legs. He bucked about a bit, but he'd once come fifteenth at a rodeo and so thought he could handle it.

"Sister Geoff!" screamed Amanda. "Do your stuff!"

And that was where the whole plan came to a crashing halt, so to speak, as Sister Geoff hadn't the foggiest what she was supposed to do. "Ghuy'cha' qagh Sopbe'!" she bellowed.

"Is that fucking *Klingon*?" said Freddy.

"Whatever it is," said the mayor, almost losing control of Pigface's left foot – the one made famous by…oh, we've done that one already – "it's not working!"

Amanda looked expectantly up at the nun, who looked down confusedly upon Amanda and shrugged. "I didn't think we'd actually catch up to the bastard," said the nun. "I thought you'd all get killed and then I could piss off back to the convent to live out my days as a semi-celibate ruffian."

"Now's not the time for *dreaming*," said Amanda. "We've got one shot at this, one chance to send this bacon-flavoured bastard back to Hell, and we're wasting it! Now pissing hurry up and do something"

Sister Geoff took a deep breath, then immediately wished she hadn't for her flatulence was playing merry hell with her today. "What did you just say?" she said.

"What? Bacon-flavoured bastard?"

"No, *after* that," said Sister Geoff.

"Wasting it?"

"After *that*," said the nun.

"Pissing hurry up and…why are you *smiling*?"

And the nun *was* smiling, and it was a good smile, and God saw that it was a good smile and so took a quick picture before the opportunity was lost. "Hold that bastard still," said the nun. "I've drunk a lot of punch and I've got an idea."

"Well whatever it is," said Freddy, wrestling the axe away from the lunatic. "I can't hold him much longer!"

"Do it!" screeched Amanda.

LARRY II: THE SQUEEQUEL

And so Sister Geoff did it. And *how* she did it would go down in history (at least in some parts, where they had nothing better to talk about). She pulled her knickers down, stepped over Pigface, and squatted.

"Ew, what the fu—" But Freddy didn't get a chance to finish as Pigface's fist connected a good one with his jaw, loosening a few teeth and giving him a temporary lisp. "Ith alright!" he said. "I've got him!" And he grabbed onto Pigface's arm once again, this time pinning it with his knee.

"She's going to piss on him!" said Mayor Ketchum.

"Holy water!" said Amanda. "Whatever passes through her comes out as holy water."

"Doesn't someone have to bless it first?" said Freddy.

"Will you lot be quiet," said the nun. "And turn your heads away. I'm not proud of this."

They did as they were told and, a moment later, a torrent did gush from the nun. Now, they say you can tell a person's diet from the colour of their urine. If it is clear, you're drinking just the right amount of water; if it is bright orange, you are at risk and might need to see a doctor; it it's red, chances are it's not blood, but last night's beetroot.

"Why's it purple?" said Freddy, sneaking a look.

"Never mind that," said the nun, forcing more piss from her system. "Look!"

And they all looked down at Pigface, who was screeching and writhing like never before. Not only that, but now a thick smoke was rising from the body. "It's working," said Amanda. "I don't believe it. It's fucking working!"

Pigface was bucking as hard as he could, and yet he couldn't shake off those holding him in place. "The power of Christ compels you!" said the nun, more for dramatic effect than anything else. The pig mask, still trying to reform, began to melt. There was a horrible rubbery smell, like burning tyres, and one of Pigface's feet came loose in the mayor's hand.

"I think I'm going to be sick," said the mayor, examining the foot – the left one, made famous by…and so on and so forth – before tossing it down the corridor. "Is he dead yet?"

Sister Geoff stopped urinating for a moment and wafted the smoke away with her hand, the one with HATE written across the knuckles. "If he's alive, he's a bloody good actor."

Just then, and all of a sudden, Freddy lost

control of Pigface's right hand – not famous by any stretch of the imagination – and it clamped around Sister Geoff's throat, squeezing tightly. Luckily, the nun still had some piss left in the pipe, and she forced it out as hard as she could.

"SQUEEEEEEEEEEE!" said Pigface as his hand fell away from the nun's throat. "Squeee-*youbastards*-eeeeee!" he also said, which was remarkable, really, considering his face looked like something you could order at a Korean takeaway.

"Go to Hell!" said Amanda.

"Yeah, what *she* said," added Freddy.

A minute later, all that remained of Pigface was a bloody and piss-soaked apron, a melted and piss-soaked pig-mask, and a rusty and piss-soaked axe.

"Everybody freeze!" said a voice, and through the smoke came the Wallowiczes, guns drawn, brows furrowed. "I hope you've got a license for that urinating nun."

"Not like you guys to be late," said the mayor.

Bobwallowicz shot him in the leg.

28
Outside the Hunter Mansion

If this were a film – which it isn't, and probably never will be – soft music would be playing over the top of the heroes as they milled around, being interviewed by the press and authorities. Parked at the end of the driveway was a solitary ambulance. Next to that was a coroner's van, which was already filled to capacity with mutilated bodies and severed limbs. Harry Hunter was talking to a pretty reporter, no doubt trying to coax her into appearing in a forthcoming production. She was, however, a consummate professional, and only agreed to appear in *Cockmunchers III* if the price was right.

Standing just outside the entrance to the mansion are our heroes, and it is here that we join them for a final bit of nonsense before this story draws to a close.

"I can't believe it's over," said Amanda.

"I can't believe I saw a nun take a piss," said Freddy.

"Yeah, sorry about that," said Sister Geoff. She wasn't, though. Not really.

"Well, I'm just glad everything worked out in

the end," said the mayor, who was just glad everything worked out in the end. He was sitting on a deckchair while a paramedic saw to his leg wound. "I always knew Haddon would be put on the map. I never imagined it would be because of an undead mass murderer."

"Do you think people will believe us?" said Freddy. "About Pigface, I mean?"

"I don't think *I* believe us," said Amanda. "But you never hear about the aftermath, do you? All that explaining to the police, and whatnot, sort of gets forgotten."

"In that case," said Sister Geoff, "do you think they'd notice if I scarpered? I'm due back at the nunnery. Don't want to be late for heavy metal night."

Amanda searched the vicinity for the Wallowiczes. "I'm sure they'd understand," she said. "Nuns are very busy people, what with all the praying and not having sex and stuff. If they ask, I'll let them know where to find you."

Sister Geoff turned to Freddy. "You owe me some weed, Escobar."

Freddy laughed.

"I'm not joking, you prick."

Freddy stopped laughing and took to farting.

"Thanks again, Sister Geoff," said Amanda, and the nun scarpered sharpish.

"Well, all's well that ends well," said Mayor Ketchum.

"That's a terrible line to end the story on," said Amanda.

"What happened to the secondary characters?" asked Freddy. "That supermodel and her moose friend?"

A screech of tyres from the road beyond the mansion gates was quickly followed by the squealing of twisting metal and two nasty sounding thuds (one slightly louder than the other), proving once and for all that it didn't pay to be a minor character in genre fiction.

LARRY II: THE SQUEEQUEL

29

"Oh no, you di-n't"

The ambulance tore through the streets, its casualty a rather large fellow missing a foot. His left foot, in fact, made famous by—

"We're losing him!" said the paramedic, a guy by the name of Hicks.

The second paramedic, Hudson, began pumping the footless man's chest. "Damn it, man, not on my watch!" said he. And then in the next breath: "Oh, he's gone." He ceased CPR. It was a waste of energy, according to the flat-line running across the screen of the beeping machine to their right. Best to chalk this one up to a bad day at the office. After all, we all have them.

"Hang on a jiffy," said Hicks, pointing to the machine, which had ceased its incessant beeping. "I believe we have a live one."

And a live one they did have. The bald gorilla with the missing foot had started breathing again. Not only that, but it looked like he was trying to say something through his oxygen mask.

"Hang on, buddy," said Hudson, removing the oxygen mask so that he could better hear. "What are you trying to say, mate?"

And the footless man said one word and one word only, and that word meant not a jot to the paramedics in the back of that ambulance, who were too busy wondering what they were having for tea to make anything of it.

"Squeee…" grunted the artist formerly known as Dee.

Squeee indeed.

THE END
(Until next year…)

www.ingramcontent.com/pod-product-compliance
Ingram Content Group UK Ltd.
Pitfield, Milton Keynes, MK11 3LW, UK
UKHW042002230426
12048UKWH00009B/491